OBSESSED

OBSESSED
two novels

STUART'S PIECE
and
BLOCK'S SPARTANS

H.L. STRYKER

The SeaHorse Press
New York City
1984

Library of Congress Cataloging in Publication Data

Stryker, H.L., 19---
Obsessed: Two Novels
1. Stuart's Piece
2. Block's Spartans

ISBN 0-933322-18-6 LC—83-51374

The SeaHorse Press, 307 West 11th St., N.Y.C., N.Y. 10014

OBSESSED

OBSESSED

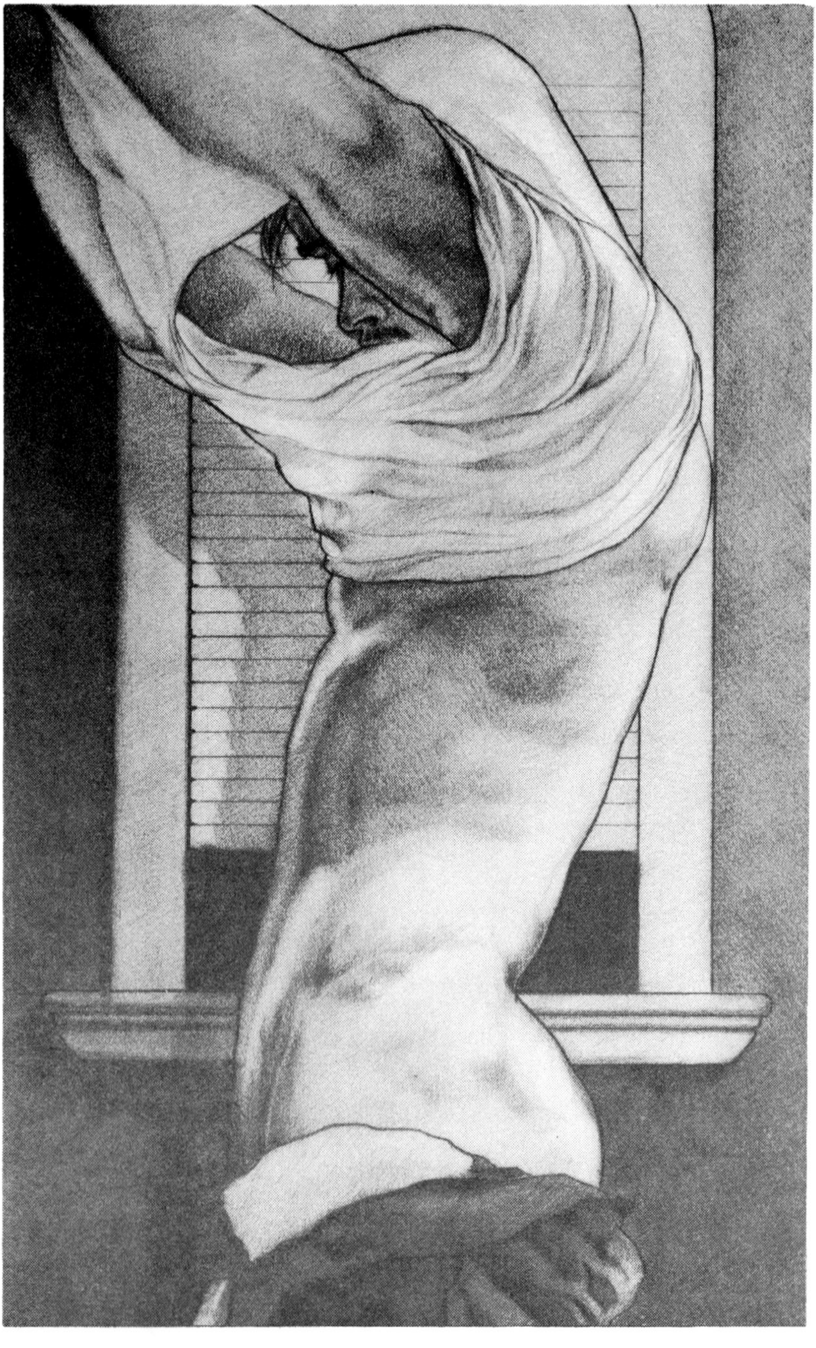

STUART'S PIECE

ONE

You've insisted we take some coke together, just the two of us ... but not with your wife, Babs. It's her heart condition, she says, which keeps her off it. Could it instead be fear of the hysteria she's at the brink of so often? Why should she live in panic's grip? She got what she wanted and has kept it these two decades, kept

YOU, your body, your peppy, eternal phallus, peppy because it's always up in my memory, memory being as much of eternity as I can possess.

By the way, if Bab's heart is so bad, why doesn't her doctor advise a diet, get her to drop some fat? If she doesn't mind having gone to blubber, aren't you offended?

You've told me you've never cheated on her, and I believe you, though, of course, you've had philandering daydreams but you don't dally with the guys after work, don't make excuses to go roaming, instead are home every evening, enthroned, watching the evening news, not that there's much of interest to see or hear, but you're home playing head of the household at the supper table with mock butch manners. We all know you take sick leave from the factory as often as you can, not that you're sick, for you're still as healthy as a stud in prime—but you are laid back, oh, so nicely, suckably laid back, on days off stripping down to T-shirt, baggy boxer trunks and sandals, in the backyard to soak up San Diegan sun from noon to sunset alongside the ordinary garden Babs has tended, the two of you as often as not doing a barbecue, drinking, you beer, she wine, always sharing the best grass—lazy, hazy. Jesus, she should know by now you're thoroughly domesticated and won't flee.

On more than one of my visits, you've repeated. "You and me should have some coke together. You'll love it."

"Have you had much of it?" I ask, concerned.

A smile deftly evades the question. "Just believe me. It's great. You, of all people, will go ape for it. And you should have it with me, because we've got a lot to talk about."

My gorgeous hunk of a guy, do you have any idea what a torrent of words might ensue? Do you have any idea how much I have to say on the subject of

YOU, how I might, in nostalgia's glow, croon of the remembered pornographic delights of

YOU all night? Are you sure the risk should be run? Remember what happened last time I was down on a visit wanting to go down on you? We might have made it, except for Babs' attack of screaming meanies.

She won't snort coke but does drag on joints like a champ, sharing one with you on the hour every hour, oftener from noon to technicolored dusk, those great breasts of hers raised as she sucks in and swallows smoky draughts. A moment later, she resumes her grating chatter, telling me at length about her eldest daughter (by a previous marriage) who is now married and living in Oregon, or some such place, going on, telling me then about her second daughter's bastard baby girl (the two of you childless). I wish I could say her tone is dulcet or that she speaks with the elegance of a Katherine Hepburn—how much happier that would be for you—but she grates, sounding as if she's on the verge of a crying jag. But what has she got to crack-up about? You don't cheat on her or beat her. Once a day you may growl and threaten to leave, but doesn't she know it's an idle threat? You'd think all the marijuana together with all the years of sleeping with

YOU, nude you and your seven- to eight-inch pacifier would have absolved the pent up hysteria in the poor dear.

The photographs she is showing to me are of her first daughter's wedding, however her hectic tone of voice is the same she used when telling me of—rather than a festive occasion—her cancer scare and hysterectomy twenty-five years ago, so you'd think she'd be over her fears by now. Happily you come to my rescue and bark, "Woman, he's not interested in hearing all that. You're boring the shit out of him. Isn't it time you got your ass inside and started fixing the stuff for our dinner?"

Her reply is screeched. "Oh, I've got such a good meal planned for the two of you. I've done one of the Ukrainian dishes Nickie's mother used to do for him."

You point the way of her exile, mock ferocity on your brow. "Woman...."

She huffs, puffs, then waddles into the house. I wish I could say she moves with the poise of a Maria Tallchief, that grace reigns in every fiber of her body, but, alas, she waddles, her face appearing as if she's about to weep, while repose comes to yours after the little flare-up, and we are alone for a half hour. But, in the kitchen, while she dices celery or whatever for whatever she has in mind to set before us, does she eavesdrop through the window screen? Does she fearfully fret we might begin reminiscing about times past

YOU then a feisty Canadian, self-dispossessed from homeland, serving in the USMC, which you'd joined on a lark, and I a more than hospitable native in a southern clime. Though you'd probably rather die than admit any of the salacious details, which by now may be blurred in your memory, Babs knows I seduced that young leatherneck, in spite of himself, and knows too it was me—your buddy Stu—that Nick Blazhkov almost chose, instead of her, when your hitch was finally up and you were footloose again. California sunshine and congenial beaches had wooed you too, so you had no inclination to return to Winnipeg's bitch winters and had a decision to make: either try your luck with me or a then somewhat trim cocktail waitress named

Babs. But she had two kids (by a previous marriage) to be raised, one hardly out of diapers, an irksome complication for a guy at twenty-five, and you'd learned it wasn't so awful living with a queer, and anyway you still had a lot of wild

CUM to sow.

You say we've got a lot to talk about. Well, even though I don't approve of the junk, maybe you should bring out the coke for us to snort, and I'll tell you what I know now (years too late) what I should have done that morning after our last night in bed together, should have done all through the morning and afternoon to let you know you were the phallic object of my affections. Want to hear explicitly? Dare I tell? Babs is in the kitchen, within earshot.

Does she peek out to see if I'm getting aroused by the sight of you? Bright light and shadows of leaves have formed a filigree upon your biceps; your brow too, which is only faintly tanned in spite of your sun worshipping, a fluttering filigree also upon your forelegs and crotch. By the way, how come you haven't gotten fat? Isn't Babs' blubber contagious? You're almost as sinewy as the night you first dropped your drawers for me.

I gaze at your mustachioed face, which reminds me of pictures I've seen of fierce, wooly, blond Cossacks, the kind of face a Russian writer says we'll never see the likes of again; an honest, unneurotic, robust face. While we, avoiding the real issues, distractedly talk of politics and the state of the world (which gets worse each year it seems) you wear sunglasses, so I don't see the puffy crow'sfeet around your eyes, oncoming old age taking form like a specter. However, even when you've removed the shades, when your face is naked, I see past the years, see it as it was at twenty-four, taut under a crewcut; you kind of a cross between Jeff Bridges and Nick Nolte. When I saw Bridges in *The Last Picture Show,* I could hardly think of anyone but you for days, though we'd been separated for years. Even later, when I saw Nolte in the *Dallas Cowboys,* I dreamed of you all night, and for days seemed obsessed with the memory of the night of our first meeting, on Christmas Eve in a festive bar, where servicemen, broads and a smattering of queers sported in the season's cheer. "Merry, merry, Goddamn Christmas," the drunken, young sailor greeted, as he happily advertised his endowment at an upstairs urinal. But I'd already set my sights on you across the noisy room below, sent you and your two buddies a round of drinks, telling the waitress to keep the buyer anonymous, though on the second round she blabbed, and you came through the jostling tangle to meet me, smiling, extending a hand, saying, "Let me be the first to shake the hand of the last of the big time spenders," your manner buoyant with a butch mirth which swept me off my feet.

While it wasn't love at first sight, it was unabashed lust, I so eager to have my appetite whetted, wetted by

YOU, I ran the risk of serious trouble when I invited, not only Nick Blazhkov, but also his two chums to my beach apartment, a reckless thing to do, considering the three of you were strangers, jarheads, so-called tough guys and trained killers. But I couldn't pry you from them, and, caution to the wind, it was the season to be jolly, the night for peace on earth and goodwill to men, particularly horny young men, particularly

YOU.

There was a double bed in my bedroom, also a double hide-a-bed within the living room divan, and you gruffly took charge of sleeping arrangements, saying you'd sleep in the living room with one of your buddies—the white one of course—and I should sleep in the other room with who else but the black fellow. Did you think it proper that, if anyone had to sleep with a queer, it should be a nigger? Did you think your blond virginity would remain unsullied by both of us?

But, to get on with it, after lights were out and not a creature was stirring, not even a mouse, then the sugarplum fairy, so to speak, intrepidly rose and tiptoed into where you were bedded down, having noted the side you'd chosen. If we take some coke together, will it cut through your marijuana haze in sharp flashback? Will you remember there was no need for foreplay, that you knew exactly what was going on when I knelt at the bed's edge and lightly lifted the covering sheet and that you were ready when a hand touched your legs and felt the downy hair? In a matter of seconds, my hand brushed the

HARD-ON you had even before I whispered sweet nothings between your

BALLS.

A dropped pot clamors within the house. Is Babs having an anxiety attack, or merely reminding me of her presence? But I haven't said a thing, except nonsense about the dire state of the union. Does she read the thoughts writhing beneath my poker face. Like a Latin lover wanting to tear open his heart in renderings of passion, yet constrained, I silently repeat: you didn't recoil when I took hold of your

COCK. Need I remind you that it was into my mouth that you profusely jettisoned your semen in less than a minute?

Considering how much was to happen later, and that my lust would evolve into mutual and difficult love, it doesn't matter now that on that first night you instantly sprang from bed, pulled up your shorts, marched to the bedroom and angrily slammed the door. At least you didn't beat me up, but instead left me unharmed, unlike the poor wretch, who, that Thanksgiving, had invited two sailors to his place for a turkey dinner. They bludgeoned him to death, carved him up some, shoved his severed penis into the bird's roasting carcass, then scrawled his blood on the walls—or so the newspaper reported—the print reading *louzy c... s.....*, mispelling noted. But rather than punish me, you left me with your buddy, whom I didn't molest, though he had me feel what he had up, though he asked for a blowjob. How could I turn from you to him? Aglow as I was, transfixed by the fix you'd just given me,

YOU, my one and only that night, and for many nights to come.

For me, memory blooms without the aid of any drug, and

of course, I turn onto you again twenty years later, particularly when you, oh so casual in your garden, lift your T-shirt from time to time and pat your firm belly. Do you realize what you're doing? Or haven't you sensitivity enough to know how that gesture taunts me? Do it again and I may cross over to you, lower those trunks slowly over your thighs, past the chunky

PRIZE. If you don't know, Babs understands well enough, for, in the kitchen ... the pot is dropped a second time.

Frankly, we ought to cut this visit short. On my last one, you and I almost made it, but it got wrecked.

The hotel room was my idea but I had no idea it would create such a tacky scene. I'd only said when phoning, "Yes, I'm coming down on a visit ... yes, but last time you and Babs went off to bed so early, leaving me trapped in your house without a car ... this time I'm getting myself a room in the city in case I feel like hitting the bars after you folks nod off." Of course, I didn't tell you what I actually had in mind, kept secret that only six blocks from the hotel is a certain place, in the dimly lighted corridors of which a congregation of guys wander with removable towels around the waists of otherwise naked bodies; the towels come off in cubicles, steam and sauna rooms. That's right, only six blocks away, the Baths! Off and on for five years, I've gone to this torrid hang-out, catching Amtrak in L.A. and coming to San Diego, not visiting you but instead checking into that club around nine in the evening and remaining until the first return train in the morning. Of all such places in the Golden State, I'd chosen this one because of its proximity to MCRD, where you got your recruit training in the Corps, you and thousands upon thousands of other bucks. Also because of its proximity to naval stations and docked ships, back from the high seas. A good many sailor and marine strays take advantage of the special rates given to servicemen—and not just for a steam bath, but instead to get some hardcore affection. And I must confess to having a sixth sense for finding lively rough trade, even in half light. It's something in their manner as they sit about waiting to be approached but only in the right way, rejecting anyone who makes the slightest wrong move, anyone who doesn't know exactly where and how they want to be touched. So anyway, without meaning to go into a dissertation, there I was, often enough, not four miles from where Babs had you nude in bed, not six miles from my former beach pad where you'd given me a Yuletime fix—in the Baths, inspired by Jeff Bridges and Nick Nolte movies, blowing a variety of studs over the years, savoring the prime meat of America off farms, out of cities and down from the mountains, but often thinking of sucking only

YOU.

Anyway, having the room in town was my idea but I had no idea the two of you would check into the adjacent room. I doubt it was Babs' doing; probably yours. Were you yearning for a little adventure? Did you mean it when you said on the phone, "If you're going to hit the bars, can I come with you?" Did you have a yen to reminisce with me in our old haunts?

Whatever. It was a pleasant enough afternoon, in spite of the lady's grating yapping. I simply turned her off as the three of us sat, fourteen floors up, half out of the room and half on the balcony under an idiot blue sky. Joints were passed, chablis drunk, the warm air idle, the view of the bay cinemascopic, a mosaic of blue-silver glint and white pleasure boats, and you, looking (at least in my mind's eye) splendid when you went to the edge and leaned forward, forearms and elbows supported by the railing as you scanned the scene, sunlight drenching you and your

RUMP, well shaped, the cloth of your casuals clinging to the two oh-so-kissable mounds.

Stop the action. Flashback to our second sexual collision.

Though you'd glowered contempt at me Christmas morning for what the sugarplum fairy had done, the following New Year's Eve, in the same bar, you were friendly enough, contagious high spirits again. You said you didn't want me buying you drinks this time, and added, "But I gave it some thought, Markham, and decided you're probably an okay guy ... except you should get over that crap. You know what I mean ... You should hate it as much as I did." So I kept my hands to myself that night and went home alone, greeting the New Year with sadness. However, three weeks later, one stormy night, you, I and a friend of yours got fairly well-oiled in Tijuana, and, because you didn't have the money or inclination to try any of the cheating, Indian whores there, because too it was pouring cold rain and you had no place to go, except the base which you said you hated, perhaps more than what I'd done to you, you agreed to take shelter in my place. "Just as long as there's no funny business."

But you started it.

Your drunken buddy had thrown up out my car window, then again in the bathroom. While you cleaned up after him, I went out to skinny-dip in the storm, feeling utterly extravagant, and nearly drowned in a riptide of black, rain-lashed waves. But I wasn't about to allow myself to die, neither ingloriously nor in divine madness. Not that night, since I was sure

YOU would be waiting for me.

After being beached by a wave and then letting my heart settle from panic, I got up and, feeling sanctified by this brief brush with death, went up to where you indeed waited. Your friend had crashed on the pulled out hide-a-bed. You were still up, shoes, socks and shirt off. After one glance at my nakedness, you walked to the open bedroom doorway, turned, grunted, and said; "You look like a drowned rat. Get your skinny ass in here."

Babs, before I go on with this, you may want to cover your ears, or do you prefer to hear how dumbfounded I was when I saw Nick, our guy, dropping his britches, then shorts, when I saw him cast in a light suddenly adazzle, saw him turning to show me the seven- to eight-inch, rotund

COCK which had sprung

straight out from him. To tell you the truth, I've never seen anyone so stark naked in my life and, over the years, have always thought of him at that moment as a bolt of blond lightning in a Ukrainian or Canadian sky, the memory of him eternally crackling in my mind.

Needless to say, my heart was racing again with joy. I wildly, blindly threw myself at him in confusion, and, Babs, do you care to hear how we were presently arranged in the mystery of animal attraction?—would you believe, smooching lips to puckered anus? I don't know what they do up in Winnipeg on winter nights, but if no one had ever done this to him before, he caught on with uncanny quickness, bending over, yanking the buns apart, letting me avidly have at the morsel, which was (still is, I hope) the color of milk chocolate. Honest, I hadn't schemed to do this, hadn't even known I desired it, but there I was lapping away in primordial hunger, he shoving his handsome butt onto my face, the underside of his psyche bared to the light, the sweet orifice responding, dilating, and, one craze leading to another, there I was, in the course of human affairs, with half of my dick presently in Nick Blazhkov's ass.

But, Babs, let me reassure you. Your man wasn't about to take that, not that night, anyway. He grumbled fiercely, broke away and, after another confusion of limbs, turned the matter around, roughly working to impale me and of course without first coaxing the hole with kisses, as I had done in grace to his. So there I was, a fool without a lubricant, with a hot marine doing his best to fuck me, and, as you can imagine knowing the size of his tool, the pain was terrific. I flailed like the proverbial stuck pig. Taking it as long as I could I finally rearranged us, got him laid back and took his impetuosity in the head. He climaxed almost immediately thereafter, and, Babs, you'll be glad to hear that your hubbie then speedily retrieved his clothes, bolted from me and the room, slammed a door and hit the sack next to his unconscious buddy. All in all, we'd been at it probably less than ten minutes.

I wonder where your wife has gone, Nick. Has she jumped off the balcony?

But no, we were sitting in a restaurant. Having smoked

grass and drunk wine from two in the afternoon to seven, we were still not inebriated. Perhaps the long day's warmth had evaporated the booze, though we were happily adrift and alone. Where was Babs? She'd gotten angry over I don't know what. Perhaps because I wasn't listening to what bristled between you two in the *China Camp,* where, our appetites made ravenous by pot, we were having rice seasoned with onions and bacon, chicken breast cooked in cherry brandy and a dish of sweet baby back ribs, along with another bottle of *Fumé Blanc.* Then the two of you suddenly began squabbling over a trifle, an old gripe, the way married couples do. She huffed and puffed out, taking a cab back to the hotel, leaving us alone. You made light of it, shrugged your shoulders when I asked what went wrong. Later, in the annex bar, Fat City, surrounded by potted ferns and a cascade of Tiffany glass, the two of us alone at last, out on the town, retracing steps taken when you were twenty-four and I twenty-nine, you, my dear man, got more mellow, got further laid back. Was this it? Were we going to make it for old time's sake?

There was reason for me to be encouraged. At the end of my previous visit, while you were walking me to the train, I briefly spoke to you of my resurrected affections, saying, "Nick, there's only one thing I really regret about my life."

"Yeah?"

"It's that I didn't spend more of it with you ... that we let too many years go by without..."

You interruped and seriously said, "But I figured that's the way you wanted it."

"Not exactly. I thought I was staying away those years for your sake ... so you could have *your* kind of life."

Had we imperfectly communicated? At the moment, it didn't matter, for you unexpectedly gave me a kiss on the back of my neck. Not a fleeting kiss but a big smooch, right there in the sunny depot, before a throng. So perhaps our love hadn't been lost, but was only dormant until another glorious San Diego day when we were forty-five and fifty, in a cocktail lounge less than two miles from where we first met, the low lights softening our faces, our gazes, you getting oh so congenial in a deep, velvety chair. Wish it were a love seat.

What are you saying? That we should take some coke together. "Because you and me have got a lot to talk about."

Yes, indeed. Before touching your knee in exactly the right way, I'd like to remind you of the letters I wrote to woo you back. Remember? After our second hasty coupling, you didn't show up for how long? Two months? But I was only somewhat daunted. Having your address at base, I began writing

HAIL, BLAZHOKOV! Hola! Though you've kept out of sight these past few weeks, you figure stunningly in memory here. It isn't forgotten that you've grown stalwart from a kernel of golden Ukrainian wheat, which your father planted in Canada. Though you're temporarily out of sight, not out of mind, it's a delight to visualize you jaunty on the horizon here in imagination, again and again. However, fancy finally only teases. Your actual presence would be like creation taking shape out of the void—not a big man, true, but firm of shoulder and limb, sturdy of leg and thigh, and the cove below my place would welcome you to sunbathe and swim. The gulls would be more buoyant in flight and the crashing waves more playful if you were here to ride them.

HAIL, BLAZHKOV again. Though you may have several aces in the hole, several portals to enter from storms, here's a key to another door. It's your easy smile and jovial face which is seen most sharply in memory, though God knows you can be stern when riled. I don't regret that you were angered, for what good would your cheer be if you couldn't also express indignation. What was done had to be done, since we rushed to do it. But, remembering the manly, free-spirited openness of your face. I believe surely you've overcome resentment by now. Just as daylight is more expensive than night, so mirth and lust are bigger than rancor.

The rack of lamb cooked here last Sunday for friends would have been better served if you had been at the head of the table to carve it. How much happier the evening would

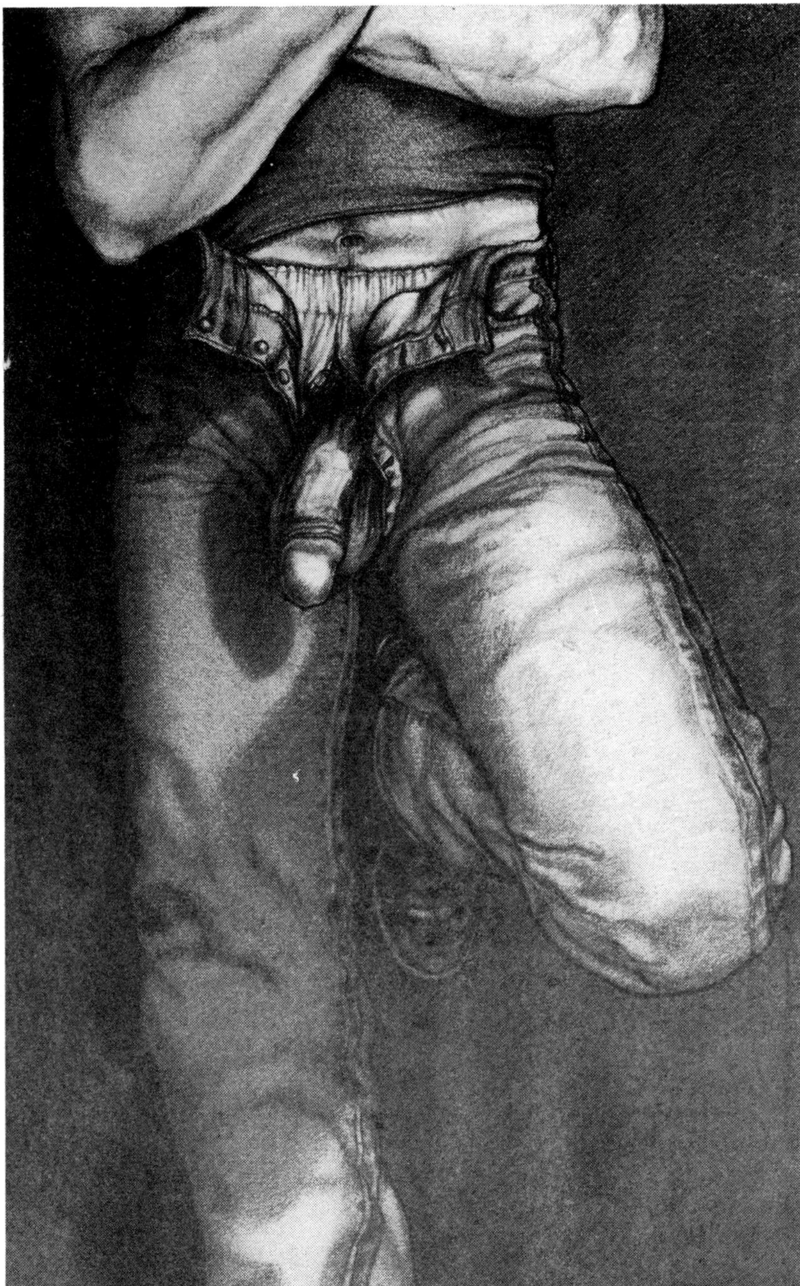

have been if you had been here having your fill of food, drink, music and laughter, and if, after the guests had departed, you had settled back in a home away from home. Good Lord, a man grown virile from the best wheat, a man with Cossack blood in his veins, Russian sperm in his loins, shouldn't be beset with hesitation. Come—enjoy this part of the world too—use the key at your whim.

"Did you mind me sending the letters?" I asked when we next met. After a moment's thought, you replied, "No ... everyone likes hearing his name sounded out at mail call. It makes you feel important," which is exactly what I'd wanted you to feel and still do, my good man.

"Kind of crazy letters," you added and, your sense of humor alive, you said you'd shown the key to a few of your buddies on base, spoofing them, telling them it was to the door of some beautiful, rich dame's pad. So there we were, reunited, sharing a private joke, obviously glad to be in one another's company.

However, the occasion wasn't entirely carefree. You assumed a very heavy tone, saying there was something you had to tell me, taking a while to get it out. But when you did the information was clear enough: you were of the opinion that I'd given you—of all things—the clap. The clap! "That's right. About a week after ... after you know what ... well, the whanger starts dripping. After tests were taken, the medic patted me on the shoulder and congratulated me on being the father of a big dose."

The clap! Thunder!

"From me? Blazhkov, no way."

"What else could I figure? It was only about seven or eight days after..."

"Don't you think I'd know if I had any such thing? And what do you think I am ... some gonococcus-Mary running around giving marines clap? No, sir, if it was clap you had, you got it from someone else, perhaps one of those whores in T.J. ... Not from yours truly, and if you don't believe me, I'll take every V.D. test known to medical science, and if I'm not as clean as … as…"

You interrupted with laughter, almost cracking up.

"What's so damn funny?"

It was a moment before you caught your breath. "Markham, I wish you could see your face. Shit, man, you're so fucking mad your nostrils are flared at least an inch wide. I've never seen anyone look so mad." Laughter again. Your face reddening again.

What was important was that you were in good spirits, and we were reunited, to go on from there. I remained in a sulk for a time, as we drank more than our share, my injured pride on the mend. The two of us went to one of those dilapidated places where old, blue movies were shown, watched jerky, grainy images of two Latin ladies at cunnilingus, then taking turns fellating some hung, greasy-haired dude. Sitting in Fat City twenty years later, you more relaxed in the pale apricot glow of a Tiffany lamp, my all-time-favorite stud is saying, "It's too bad we don't have some coke. Too bad people can't take it in public, in a pretty place like this. 'Cause we would have a great old time." Should I remind you how one other evening drew to a close? As we drove home, I didn't know if the skinflicks had aroused you or not, but I'd sworn I wouldn't touch you, not with a ten-foot pole, since you'd accused me of spreading gonorrhea. On our return home, with none of your buddies along to complicate matters this third time, you seemed to have forgotten the clap, if that's what you'd had, and you made no move to pull out the hide-a-bed, but instead undressed in the bedroom. You got between the sheets of my bed without saying a word, while I, meaning to keep my word, remained up, saying I was going to read. Can you imagine?

How long did I let my eyes toss in the jumble of black marks? Twenty minutes? Probably no more than ten before I joined

YOU, and, no sooner had I touched pillow than you, awake and vibrant, reached over, took hold of my right hand and drew it to….

But you're saying it's too bad people can't snort coke in public. I'm thinking it's a shame, since your trousers are beltless, since you lift your shirt, show some navel and pat your belly twice, perhaps not meaning to entice me, perhaps merely enjoying your body's sensuality in idleness—and since the body of a man in health is still a wonder to my reckoning, and some of us rejoice in sharing a guy's sexual excitability, well, because of all that, it's too bad I can't get you naked here amid Tiffany splendor as I would in the Baths. I'd be proud to have a small audience watch me repeat what I did that night when you hastily drew my hand to your

WHANGER, as you called it,

that hard handful you had waiting for me in the dark, the sheet thrown back and my head in place, down on you, to receive what was welling up. That third time the two of us coupled long enough for my succulent zeal to manifest itself with saliva flow, and then there was the rush or your Cossack

CUM. Among other things we

could discuss, I could remind you that there was no angry desertion that time, no slammed door. You remained with me in the slumber and I found repose, having had a psychological, perhaps even a spiritual orgasm.

It's last call in Fat City. How many bars did we close in the old days, then go home to bed? Mightn't we do the same tonight? Your affection is even more expansive as we take to the boardwalk between the cocktail lounge and hotel. The same wharf you once jumped ship on, phoning, asking to be picked up for a night on the town, and I went to get you, and there you were in boots and military fatigues looking like almost everyone's favorite star in a war movie. And here we are again, at forty-five and fifty, the dark waters of the bay lapping at black pilings, the humid, seaside air as pungent as the remembered taste of your crotch, sentimentality abuzz in our heads, and, as you draw closer, an arm, weighty and slightly moist, is placed on my shoulders, and your voice is husky when you say, "You're a damn good buddy, Markham. Maybe the best buddy a guy ever had."

Good Lord, where oh where am I to take you?

Up to the room next to where Babs is most likely waiting, pacing in anxiety. Hardly.

The *Star of India,* a once-upon-a-time, merchant clipper, now a museum, is docked nearby. Too bad it's closed for the night, otherwise I would lead you aboard and down to a hold, where salt-spray, sun-weathered sailors of old used to sleep. How crowded were they in their bunks, in their fitful sleep? We can guess they were not always chaste, that under coarse blankets, there was stealthy, solitary hand motion, men being men with or without women. How much semen was forlornly spilled in bilge-smelly wood? Did the ship's creaking and the howling of storms cover the action of the emboldened? How many took lovers? Damn, if the ship weren't locked up, that's where I'd get you to lower your pants, surrounded by the ghosts of rough salts. Wish we'd spent our lives together on the high seas under sail. I would have gone around the world on you a thousand times.

On the other hand, it has crossed my mind that I might lead you a few blocks in the opposite direction, to a place where a pack of guys (no ghosts they) prowl in search of a partner or partners, and where, through thin cubicle partitions, can be heard the telltale slurp-slurp-slurping; where on the best nights the horny get hornier from time to time in an orgy room, lust breaks out in abandon, so that twelve to twenty would-be lovers are in a tangle, a restless, bareassed fraternity, openly, happily getting their rocks off.

Would you be horrified, disgusted as you were that Christmas Eve?

In any case, it would wreck the mood we're in: the two of us aglow with wine and pot, the air balmy, your arm still on my shoulder, the back of my neck kissed once again after you've said, "...maybe the best buddy a guy ever had."

Of course, on reflection, I must admit it may have been wishful thinking which made me hope the evening would end differently than it so badly did. We weren't footloose, and I didn't have a hideaway by the beach. Instead our steps led us to the hotel. I didn't help matters by saying, just as the lobby's glass door automatically opened, "I guess we'd better straighten up, otherwise they'll think we're a couple of gay sailors come to shack up," as if that made a difference. With you, I usually had a knack for saying the wrong thing at the perfect moment. But even if I'd kept silent, could you have, after our arrival on the fourteenth floor, stolen into my room rather than do what you did?

Which was, go to the next door and ring.

Had she fallen asleep? More likely she was there having a hysterical fat-attack.

The bell rang thrice.

You must have heard her moving about; you were saying, "Okay, woman, I know you're awake in there, so open the door." She screeched something back and your anger began to flare. Strange how your mood changed so quickly, but, on second thought, maybe not so strange, since women have had milenniums to learn how to get a man riled, and, of course, heterosexuality thrives on conflict.

The door was opened, the chain fixed in place, at the cracked opening, and the two of you instantly fell squabbling, saying I don't know what: I didn't care to hear. The tone was clear enough; the two of you sounded like two hissing cats. It's a wonder the house detective didn't rush to the scene. How tacky! When all I wanted was just, oh so elegantly, to blow you.

She didn't open the door, and rather than take the easy way and stay with me to sleep off your inebriation and anger, you wanted to get home to your own bed. You hesitated only because driving the car parked below was a risk. The San Diego police are only too glad to pick up drivers high on wine and grass. Perhaps because you decided a night in jail wouldn't be as bad as a night in bed with me, you took the chance, in your wrath leaving me without a word of goodbye, as if I didn't exist. Some way to treat the best buddy a guy ever had! But the dreadful affair wasn't quite over. My phone rang, Babs wanting to continue her gripe with you and, thereby, to disrupt any accord she no doubt feared you and I might find. After telling her you had left, I hung up, and drew the curtain. Of course, I was too weary and despondent to push the night's ill luck any further. I'd lost the knack of making the right touch at the right moment in the right place on the right guy.

TWO

That should have been the end of it. However, as life is a matter of keeping some momentum going, I had made up my mind to effect a drastic change in my life—to leave Californian shores, the land of laid-back Lotus Eaters, and move across the continent, to the tumult of Manhattan, where capitalism has run amuck and people out of necessity are ballsy. So, since three thousand miles would soon separate us, and since you and Babs wanted to buy my car, which I wouldn't need and didn't want, and since on the phone you said with enthusiasm, "I tell you, before you go, you and me should have some coke together, sit up all night, snort away and talk our heads off"; and too, given our record for *not* keeping in touch—once three years went by without contact; another time four years (since I wasn't pining for you)—well, considering all that and the distance I was about to put between us, one of us could drop into his grave without a farewell, without reminding ourselves in mutual duet of my lust for you—a lust which evolved into mutual love, a love which could speak its name but couldn't fly as one wing of that bird of love was crippled—so, why shouldn't I make one more trip? maybe take some coke with you? sit up all night, and maybe have the gumption to tell you you're a low-life jerk for leaving me in that hotel room without a word of goodbye, as if our sentimental evening had meant nothing more to you than—than what? An old, black and white, late, late movie you watch in doldrums?

On the other hand, I might try, outspokenly, to remind you of our erotic times past, though your memory may have atrophied. Could it be revived with mouth-to-cock resuscitation? Remember? after that night when you drew my hand under a sheet, that night you didn't leave my bed, and thereafter used the key, showed up almost every weekend for a year and better, my Friday-Saturday-Sunday-displaced-young-marine-husband? It surprised me how much you enjoyed shopping with me for the weekend's food, enjoyed supervising in the kitchen as I prepared Sunday spreads; the two of us having a few of my friends over, "just as long as the queers keep their hands to themselves," you said. And they did, in awe of you and of my success in keeping such a studsy number. The Korean War was over and the USMC wasn't sending aliens—displaced Canadians like you—overseas, so you were denied Tokyo and Yokohama delights, stuck in Pendleton with a bunch of leathernecks (animals you called them), stuck with my hospitality. The two of us rode waves afternoons, went to the movies evenings or caroused in beach beer-bars, laughing and scratching. I moved to a bigger place so you could have a room of your own. It had louvered French doors which closed and you had the privacy of a narrow bed. And you truly enjoyed my patio of plants where you husbanded philodendrons,, ferns and begonias, as the hi-fi played—not my usual Mahler and Mozart—instead Elvis and Little Richard, records I'd bought for

YOU, you keeping your crew-cut, butch posture, playing

ROUGH TRADE, giving me my fix, but no more than once a weekend, and, in time, you stopped telling me the mornings after how much you hated it.

As long as I've driven all the way to San Diego, perhaps for the last time, why shouldn't you be reminded of another evening. We came in later than usual. Never needing any foreplay, you half dropped your drawers before we got to the apartment door. Inside, you turned on the phono, flicked on the twinkly lights in the patio's shrubbery and began frugging and watusiing, tossing your clothes here and there, telling me how at Winnipeg parties everyone expected Blazhkov to do his number before the festivities broke up. "They didn't call me

NICK THE NUDE for nothing."

But rather than get myself agitated with remembrances of pornographic times past, it's enough to say that within less than ten minutes you were .... But no! Be still my lascivious heart.

I've read that premature ejaculations are a sign the guy really wants it over and done with, that very likely he doesn't care much for sex. In any case, after gratification you were soon asleep and I couldn't go on sucking you; I felt like a thief in the night robbing you of your repose, and so I left you in your narrow bed.

Okay, having driven the hundred miles, here I am again in your backyard, alongside the garden Babs has tended. She's on guard, her wet, frightened eyes watching. And since your memory of our past love seems to be a corpse, let's get this over with, transfer the car's registration and say goodbye. But then you're saying, "We got to snort some coke together before you take off for the Big Apple ... right?" Between Christmas and New Year's, there's hardly more than two hours of sun: the filigree of light and shadows on your flesh soon vanished. We were confined to the house, where we ate early—another one of Babs' Ukrainian dumps—and not long afterwards you, with a commanding tone, say, "Okay, woman, go get the coke. Stu and me are going to do it. Right?"

"Perhaps I don't want any," I say with annoyance.

Babs handed you a plastic bag one-quarter full of the white substance, and carefully dispensing it onto a cardboard square, you say, "Markham, you're going to *love* it."

"What effect does it have?"

You stab at the air with a tease. "It turns you into a sex-fiend."

Envisioning myself ripping your clothes off, or, better yet, you transformed into a Satyr chasing me around the table, I retort, "I doubt that Babs wants two sex-fiends charging around her house."

You quickly back off. "I was only kidding."

"Then what will it do?" Of course, I'm apprehensive, not knowing if the drug will destroy my self-control, not knowing if some two-headed, snouted, fanged monster, so to speak, will rise out of my psyche. I doubt I have one, but there are some lurking resentments.

"You won't know 'til you try." Having taken a razor blade and begun to chop the crystals, your golden-downy wrist controlling the deft strokes, you go on to say, "Of all the people I know, you're going to get the most out of it."

"Why?"

"Because of that mind of yours."

"What about my mind?"

"It's always racing a mile a minute. With coke, it's going to take off into the wild blue yonder."

"Will you be here to bring me back?"

Out of a small pile of powder, using the sharp edge of the blade, you form a thin, white line on the cardboard. Then, using a short, pink-and-white striped cocktail straw and bending your head forward, you demonstrate how the stuff is inhaled into a nostril. Then you sit back looking quite pleased with yourself, and say, "Okay, Markham, your turn now."

Studying your blue eyes to discern any suspicious change in them, I reply, "But I haven't said I was going to take any."

"You will. You've always been a good sport. I've never seen you chicken out."

Indeed! How come I backed away from our proverbial moment of truth, when you, belly down, spread-eagled on my bed, twenty years ago, offered me your magnificent...

BUT no, I told myself not to get fomenting on all that again. No, I've come to hear what you have to say, since you keep repeating how much we have to talk about.

In the dinette where we sit, you've pushed the cardboard to my side of the table and handed me the straw: a gauntlet thrown down. Under the circumstances, what else am I to do but lower my head and proceed, hoping I won't rave. Who knows, I might start bitching because you left me in that hotel room without a word of goodbye, much less a little kiss of parting. However, I risk it, do the deed, lower my head wishing it were down on something other than a chemical substance. Two snorts. There. What next? Well, except for a dry burning of nasal tissue, nothing. Certainly nothing like the transports I felt when sniffing at your...

But no. I keep still, and you take another snort, then, after forming another white line, pass it back to me. "Go on. You need more, and it takes awhile." I feel a wry smile form on my lips. If it takes awhile, as you say, what's so great about coke? I remember times when, almost as soon as we were coupled, you put me into raptures with another white substance.

After I've lifted my head a second time, your eyes search mine with whimsy, and my eyes search yours again. Two minutes. Three. Will we suddenly see flung bouquets? Four minutes, five. Still nothing.

Babs is in the living room, not seven teet away, presumably doing a crossword puzzle by lamplight, though I'm sure she's waiting to hear what we say. Well, my dear man, exactly what *do* you have to say? I wait. Is it ten or twenty minutes later that you begin telling me about your young friend, John, the fellow who supplied the coke, telling me how much money he makes pushing it, more than enough to keep him free-wheeling. He's got bags of the best Acapulco Gold stashed in your garage, along with cocaine and bags of unbanked money. By the way, could this be another cause of your wife's incipient hysteria? The poor lady afraid of a police raid? I can read it in the *San Diego Union*—LOCAL COUPLE PART OF DOPE RING; can see her tearfully waddling off to jail.

And is she jealous of your obvious admiration of this John? Frankly, if you don't stop extolling his successes, I'm likely to punch you in the mouth.

Apart from the light in the room suddenly seeming rather harsh, the first effect of the drug is the peculiar sensation of my brain tightening, as if someone is painlessly turning a big corkscrew in the center of it, turning it a bit at a time, brain fiber coiling around it ever so slowly, tightening in a coil around, I fear, a tumor of resentment, for you go on and on about this John, whomever he may be, telling me he's just about the coolest, smoothest dude you ever met: a dapper dresser, expensive clothes—a damn good coke buddy, sometimes a hilarious wildman when he's on the stuff, hot with chicks, too. Who could miss your obvious longing to emulate him, to be a rakish criminal, devilishly handsome, a dangerous Lothario.

For reasons unknown, you suddenly tell me this pusher calls Babs *Mom*.

"I hope he doesn't call you *Dad*."

"He calls me *Nick the Nude*."

Oh dear, have you performed for him? If you have, did you tell him about the night in Tijuana when you leapt onstage and out-shone the lazy, Mexican strippers under the spotlights; not only boldly flashing, but saucily mooning as well? Have you told him how, on the way home, you did a private strip for me in the rain-pelted car, tempting me first with your front side, then your beautiful, oh so kissable ....

But no, I don't want to get myself aroused thinking about that bittersweet night, for I'll either jump out of my skin or fall to weeping, since that was the crux, the bottom line, the sweet

ANUS of the matter.

Anyway, it's your turn to talk. What more do you have to say in this light that's getting harsher, crueler? It's beginning to feel like a solid weight hard on my eyeballs. Nonetheless, I tune in on you. What are you saying? Oh yes, you're talking about how much you hate your job in the aircraft factory, how you hate the hourly, daily tedium which you've put up with year after year, how much you hate the supervisorial bullshit which you've had to swallow year after year, having refused several offers of promotion to foreman yourself. Rather than whine, you maintain a butch tone of voice as you complain, asking me how a man can go on respecting himself when he goes on working at a job he hates.

"It's a damn good question, darling. First you need ask yourself what kind of work you'd like to do." This draws a complete blank. You look puzzled. Maybe I didn't get your point. Maybe you don't want to work at all. Oh dear, is this how it's going to progress? I had vaguely hoped the coke would present us with armfuls, bushels of flowers, lillies, asphodels and orchids to arrange in bouquets. Instead, you're telling me how much you hate your house, "a nigger's house," you call it. I'm gloomily surprised, for I've always had the impression you enjoyed your nest, modest as it is; roomy enough since the girls grew up and left; cozy, comfortably furnished; nothing swanky of course, but yours and probably worth five times the purchasing price, as it is only two blocks from Mission Bay.

However, on second thought, thanks to the coke, it does seem that we're sitting in a barren room illuminated by a single, naked lightbulb dangling from a long, black cord. The walls suddenly seem stark, bone white. Bones. Bones. I suppose my age is showing. Yours is, and I sense you're building up to another complaint. Are you about to tell me that you're dissatisfied with your wife? At forty-five you want a new career, a new home, a new woman or women? Good lord, have you told Babs all this, or has she sensed it? In anger—the kind of nasty anger I saw in that hotel—have you threatened to bolt? How often? If so, no wonder she has anxiety attacks. Where would the poor, fat, complaining thing be without you?

You've chopped up more of the crystals, formed another line, and taken a seventh, then an eighth snort. Again you have handed me the straw, which I use. Not because I'm getting any kick out of this cocaine—I'm not—but because we have decided to do it. We'll pursue the scene to whatever logical or illogical conclusion, which apparently will not be declaration of erotic love, but instead ruminations on your disenchantment. Sitting at this small table (its surface worn and polished, worn and polished) listening to you, should I again write love letters to woo you back?

HAIL BLAZHKOV, you are jaunty on the horizon in memory. On the other hand, since you're being so negative and this is so boring, perhaps I should remind you of Bertha.

She was fatter than Babs, weighing nearly three hundred pounds, and her awful laughter sounded as if it could rip the roof apart: maniacal as the fat-lady manikin on the pike, though some said she had a great sense of humor. How could anyone that gross from Nebraska have a sense of humor? She worked behind the bar in the Bamboo by the surf, and when she came on duty she'd bellow, "Okay, all you fags, get your heads out of your assholes, because Bertha's here to cheer you up." The woman was so heavy there wasn't so much as a dimple on either elbow. Here and there the seams of her dresses were split. Under her elephantine ankles, floorboards creaked, as did the bar when she brought down an absurdly pudgy fist. When she wasn't slinging pitchers of beer, she was putting the make on you, throwing a ponderous arm over your shoulders, drawing you to her, honey-talking you, her armpits smelling like stagnant tide pools on a sultry day. Apart from having the hots for you, she thought she was saving you from queerdom.

Since you'd been my weekend husband for several months, I figured you were probably having some kind of masculinity crisis by then. You must have been (in spite of your growing affection) sweating our one-way sex, you laid back and I aggressively down on you, sometimes twice a weekend now. What else but panic could have spurred you on to that she-walrus? In any case, I invited her over for the three of us to have a candlelit supper. She arrived in a pretty, clean dress, her cheeks rouged and her hair bobbed. Afterwards, I sent the two of you off into the night, giving you a peck on the back of your neck and thereby blessing the union. Remember? Next morning, around ten, you returned looking definitely pale, and there was a large, red hickie emblazoned on your neck only an inch from where I'd delicately kissed—a hickie, a sure sign that even walruses know passion. Well, for the next six or so weeks, our schedule changed. You went to Bertha's on Friday nights, taking your precious horniness to her, not showing up at our place until Saturday at noon, at which time our domestic accord was resumed; abbreviated. My weekly fix was denied me; not that I asked for it. How could I, since you'd dishonored yourself by slipping your shimmering clean phallus into that blubber? A friend told me I should kick you out, that I was getting masochistic. But, I must say, there were little rewards nonetheless: seeing you tend the patio plants, watching you ride a wave. And there was satisfaction knowing that it was in *my* shower that you spent twenty minutes after wallowing with Bertha. I was sure the tide would turn.

In the dinette, where the naked bulb glares on, the light striking my eyeballs which feel as if they might crack like marbles, I look at the razor blade and, feeling rather icy-hearted, think I should pick it up and take it to Babs, suggest she begin removing some fat. Not that I imagine her whacking it off, but instead making a neat incision on a thigh, so the excess lard might be worked out. If they do facelifts, how about asslifts? I won't apologize for the mean thought, nor blame it on the coke. All it has done is crystallize my feelings. And she should be called to task for allowing herself to become so gross. Sorry for the digression. What were you saying? Oh yes, something about how much money the two of us could make selling coke, like your friend John. "I mean a lot of dough, Stu," you say, and there's a scheming glint in your eyes. "Those guys you work with . . . they must need a source. I bet we could sell plenty to them."

"The guys at the corporation? Good lord, they're square; WASP executives. Their only addiction is suburban domiciles and endless TV sports. Even if they wanted to buy dope, I wouldn't sell it to them."

"How come?"

"Obvious reasons."

"Because it's illegal?"

"And other reasons."

"I remember you once liked doing something against the law, went at it like there was going to be no goddamn tomorrow."

Your sharp retort interests me. In all the years I've known you, this may be the first time you've ever thrown a cheap remark at me. Maybe it's the coke. Curious that it's you, not I who nearly dragged out our past, almost threw it on the table. Why not say in so many words—since it was against the law of the land the, my obsession to commit fellatio on you was criminal. Should I rear my head and flare my nostrils because of the contempt in your tone? Were I to address it aloud, I'd attempt eloquence. Perhaps it's sufficient to remind you that it has been legalized, in this state anyway. "You've heard of the consenting adult concept," I add, and God knows, you consented. Your cock sprung up prime of its own accord.

Your tone softens. "Maybe they'll legalize grass and coke. Thousands of people are into the stuff."

"Let them snort until they keel over, I'm not profiting on the addiction of others."

Hearing my sanctimonious tone, I inwardly cringe, want to change the subject. Since I'm not happily down on you with a mouthful, perhaps I should remind you of Vangie, the good-looking, sexy little housewife you had an affair with during your three week leave in Winnipeg. I encouraged you to go, believing you needed to return to the place of your origins to get a renewed sense of self. I even bought you a one-way ticket; you'd have to pay for your passage back. The two of us speculated whether the USMC would bother to look for an AWOL, misplaced Canadian.

"What are you trying to do, Stu—get rid of me?" you asked.

"If you decide to return, I'll be here waiting."

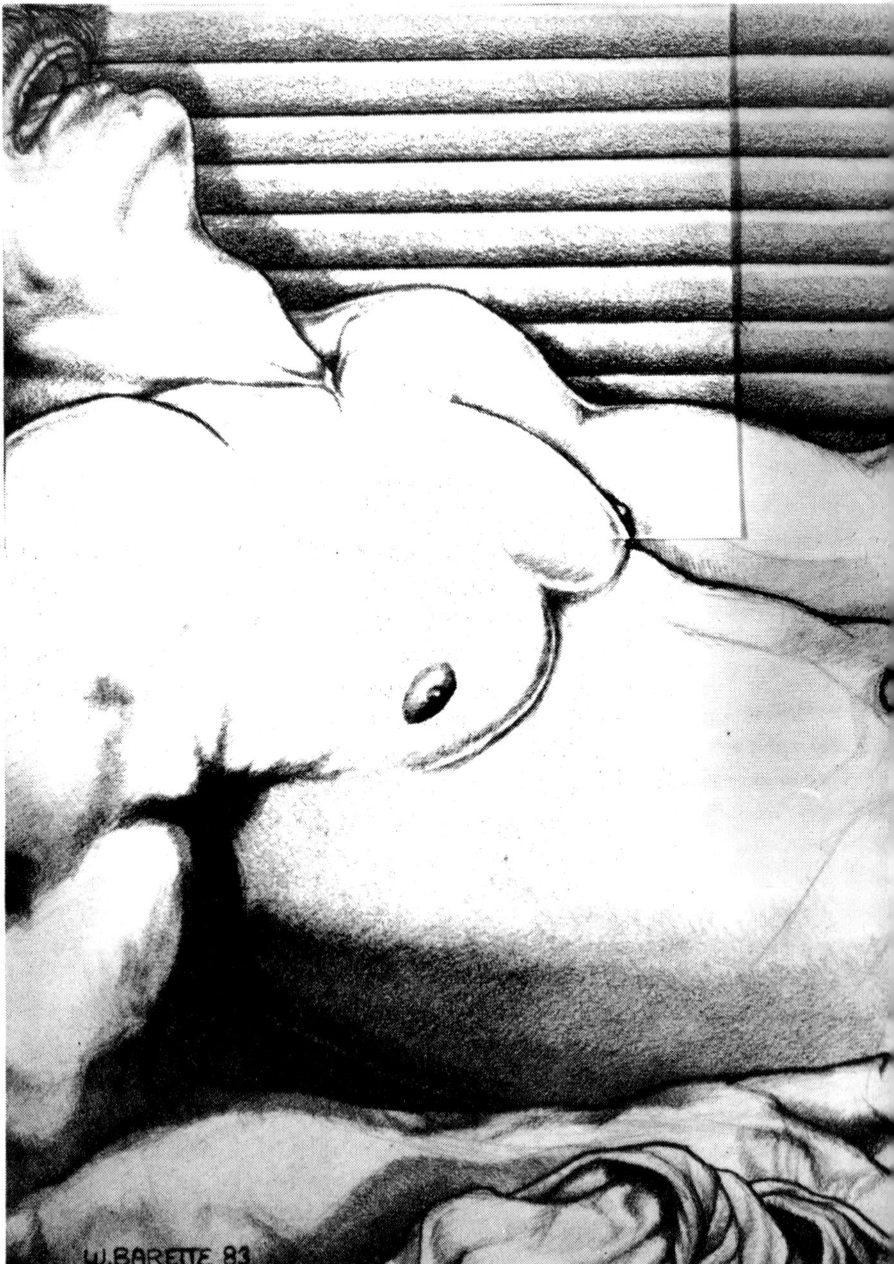
W.BARETTE 83

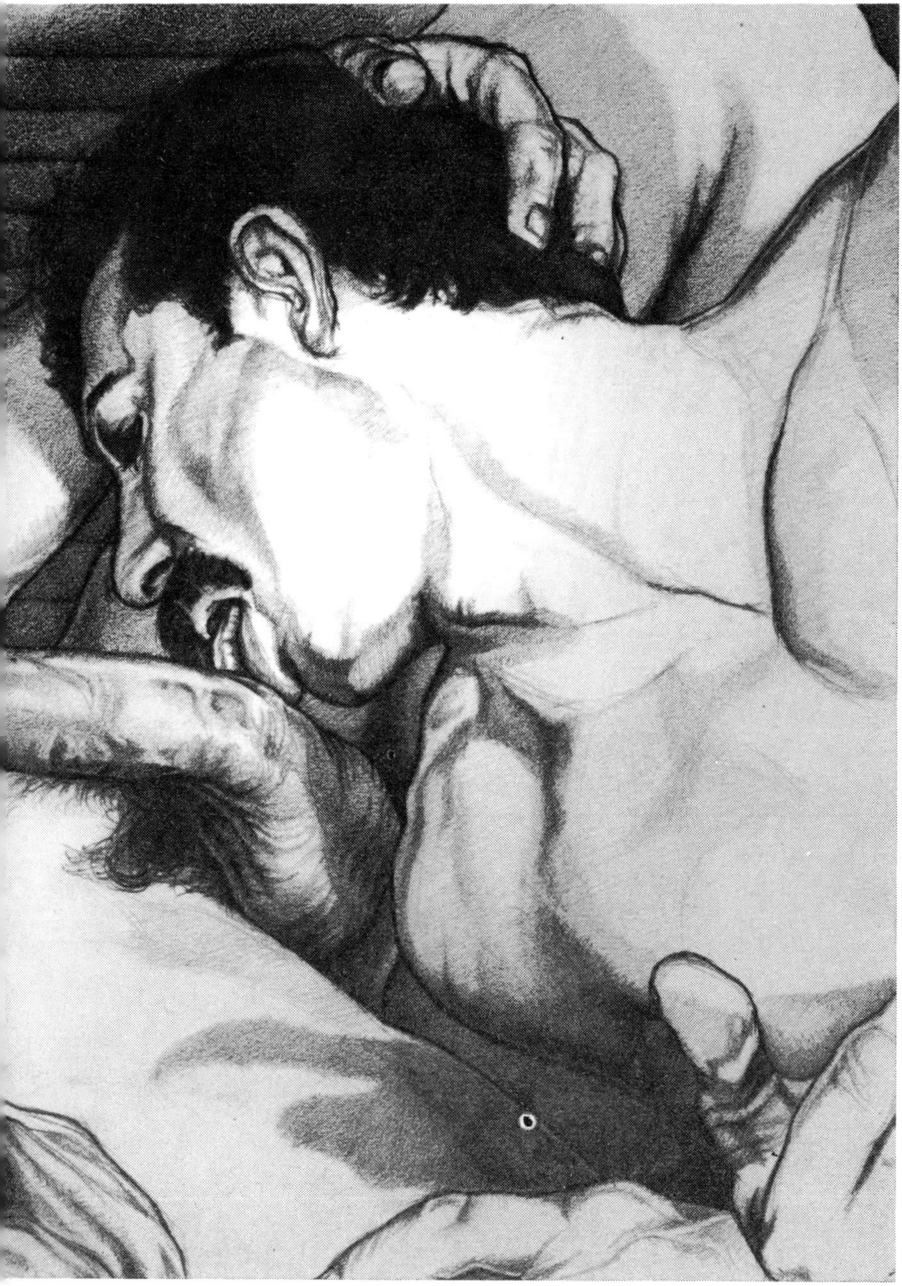

You did return, immediately telling me how you met Vangie at a party and, "It was Goddamn love at first sight." The two of you were unable to resist one another, though she was the wife of one of your former chums. Except that didn't matter, because he didn't pay much attention to his little woman, preferring to spend evenings in poolhalls with the guys. "So I could throw the whanger to her morning, afternoon and evening. I tell you, Stu, I've never had so much, and she loved it . . . the two of us screwing up a storm."

You didn't intend meanness. You weren't telling me that to get me to fly into jealous fits—which I wouldn't have done anyway—which you very well knew. No, great pride and joy filled your chest, and you had to share it with someone, needed a confidant. Who better than your devoted pal, Stu? I listened to every word and believed without doubt when you said how much she loved it. After all, even the seagulls knew I loved getting it from you. So you let the words rush out, let me in on the glorious, explicit details. Not moonlight and roses to be sure, but then I'd never asked for posy romance. Why should I? Why should Vangie, when the sight of naked you with a hard-on is enough to launch a thousand hearts to sail? Then, too, hearing that you'd fallen crashingly in love was thrilling. If you were to fall in love with *me*, would it be with such verve?

Letters flew back and forth between the two of you over the next few months. There were telephone calls from her, calls from you, at least three a weekend. I left you in privacy while you wrung out tempestuous feelings over the wires. It was Vangie this and Vangie that. You also told me how you really hated the Corps now, how you had to get back to Canada, or get yourself a good-paying job here to afford to bring her south, support her and all that. I believed if the two of you were reunited it would be something phenomenal. You'd even stopped putting the weenie to Bertha, showing up here on Friday evenings again, the home away from home I'd provided for you.

Though, of course, talking of Vangie one minute, you

couldn't very well drop your drawers for me the next, so I was still going without. Not suffering though. After all, shouldn't I want you to experience all those marvelous contradictions of a love affair, when I was nurturing such an affair for myself; since you couldn't fully reciprocate? Shouldn't I have wanted you to become a man, however you came by that manhood? You weren't getting any nookie either. Quite a fix we'd trapped ourselves into, strapped into the Platonic. But it had its rewards too.

There were smouldering undercurrents; and we would get back to the other. Maybe putting it off so long was what made it all the better. I'll never, perhaps not even in the grave, forget the night we did: the time you jumped ship before it sailed off on manuevers up the coast, the evening you called unexpectedly midweek and asked me to come pick you up, so we could have a night out on the town. "Won't you get into trouble going over the side?"

"Everyone's doing it. No one gives a shit. We don't sail until tomorrow."

What is it you're talking about now? Fixing onto your voice, I simultaneously, in my mind's eye, check to see how Babs is doing with the plastic surgery, her buttlift, and I know she's made no attempt at all to reduce, but instead steadfastly clings to her fat. I guess that's her right. Just as it is for me to trap myself in nostalgia for the way we lasciviously were. Just as it's yours to reassert how much can be made from pushing grass and cocaine, "Enough for us to quit our lousy jobs. Maybe you enjoy working your ass off, but I don't. Not at my rotten job." A moment later, you add with a lilt in your tone, "Remember how we used to talk about going to Europe together? Greece too? Well, selling coke, we could make enough to go ten times. Do nothing, sleep late mornings, see the sights afternoons, stay up late in restaurants and clubs."

I can hardly believe it. In the past twenty or so minutes—or has it been two hours—you have made reference to our past: once to my predilection for going down on you and now to how we used to daydream in unison of getting on a ship to see the world. I may have been wrong. Your memory may not be narcotized, but is instead alive and hearty. Perhaps you remember as much as I do, and both of us are keeping silent. However, I doubt that your recollections seeth as mine do. Will you let me test them openly? Here goes: "You'd had two scares ... Bertha saying she was pregnant and insisting you marry her, Vangie writing, claiming she, too, was knocked up and wanted to catch a bus to be with you in California. You turned to me in agony, 'Christ, Stu, what am I going to do? With the kind of money they pay me, I can't afford to keep a pet monkey, much less a woman with a baby in the breadbox.'

'Much less two,' I added.

'What in hell am I going to do?'

'In most cases like this, it's best to do nothing.' So you lay low in our place weekends, taking no calls. then you were scheduled to leave on manuevers. It was *me* you instantly called, after going over the ship's side for an eighteen-hour spree.

Babs, no doubt aroused by my tale, appears in the dinette on her way to the kitchen, presumably to refill her wine glass. She's listening, all right. On the other hand, you seem adrift in some reverie of your own. Your eyes, if focused, are not on me, nor on anything else in the room. I am convinced a couple under the influence of coke could never sing a duet, nor a threesome a trio—that we are on three disjunctive, solitary voyages.

So I continue in silence. Remember, once-upon-a-time buddy, how our pending remarriage was almost aborted. Prowling around in the car looking for your drunk friend—remember he'd wandered off among the city's bars—we were stopped by the cops, and, because you had no Liberty pass, they took you to Shore Patrol. That seemed the end of the adventure. Except, two hours later (I'd barely fallen asleep) the phone rang unexpectedly a second time: you telling me that after having you swab a few floors, the naval police let you go, advising you not to get into any more trouble than they would. I suppose the ebullience which graced you that evening had charmed them too. Oh happy night, it was *me* you called. Not Bertha, though she lived only six or so blocks from where they'd set you free—and then there

YOU were. Will you bother to listen if I speak again? Your wife is walking around like a somnambulist now, her incipient hysteria perhaps at rest. Why should I share what apparently is of no interest to you? There you were in my bedroom—not in the small one provided for you—removing your boots, then your military fatigues, then stretched out on *my* bed, not on your narrow one, looking like almost everyone's favorite, bareassed, AWOL Marine with a hardon, and we wedded in haste, your whanger slickened by love overflowing from my salivary glands, my throat slickened by the male emulsion flung out of your loins. We slept nude together through the remainder of that night. In the morning I was cuddling with you, feeling up your firm limbs....

BUT, stop the action! Here the story takes an even more curious turn. A sad one, raising a nagging question mark in my life, a question that has haunted me for the last fifteen years. The mystery is—since you didn't have to return to ship until three that afternoon and since I could have called into work sick (God knows as well as management, I'd given more than required)—why didn't I, that lovely morning, keep you bedded, keep you unclothed? Why didn't I arouse you again at eight, at ten, at noon again, to seek a lascivious honeymoon? To see how far we might go before you left for war games? To rationalize my hesitancy. I could say—well, you weren't responding to the cuddling, and what a man will do in the dark isn't necessarily what he'll do in the light, and there might have been slammed doors, and I didn't want to push my good luck too far, telling myself we should go on in easy stages, though God knows you were stretched out in contentment, maybe waiting for me to make the next move....

BUT I didn't, and here you are,

twenty or so years later, talking about us sharing a life of crime and leisure, getting rich and sailing off on a luxury liner. All things considered, I guess Babs would have to be included, for it would be unfair to ditch her at this late date, with her heart trouble and all. Perhaps the solution to this absurd situation would be a *menage a trois*. Rather than ask her to slice away blubber, it would be kinder to call out, "Hey, woman, let's drag this guy of ours off to bed, get him laid back between us and share him." Would that resolve this ragged malaise and bring solace to the hearts of men and fat women? On second thought, I wonder if because of her weight, the bed would be tilted in her favor so you would roll to her, not me? Well, I suppose while we're slowly crossing the Atlantic, while you lazily hump her, I could kiss your

BUTT, a rump made tough by an ice-hockey playing youth, a rump that would finally come between us. Remember, Nick—or has years of pot worn your memory to a callous?

Since we are boring each other at this dinette table, since this coke trip is a bummer, why shouldn't I rhapsodize upon your splendid ass? But first, let me set the stage for the end of the drama. I promise to be no more longwinded than you have been with your complaints. Start the action again. Bertha and Vangie in the past, the two of us reunited, separated by only two weeks of maneuvers, I drive up to Oceanside to pick you up to bring you home, and you greet me with a

HARDON. That's right, less than ten minutes after our meeting. It was a Coppertone sunset we shared as we strolled the boardwalk. You told me about the last thing I'd expected—how some Navy chief cook aboard the transport had admired your

BUNS, saying they might be the toughest in the Corps; made a few passes at them. Of course, under the crowded circumstances with your reputation threatened, you had to tell him to bug off. Which is not to say a seed had not been planted in your head. Perhaps also your heart. Judging from your buoyant tone, apparently his advances had not entirely displeased you. In any case, the tale triggered something subliminal in me. A moment later, as we ambled on, I found myself telling an inintended lie. You had asked me what I'd done while you were away. I answered, "Well, among other things, I went up to L.A., haunted some old stomping grounds and ended up in the sack with a former flame." There wasn't an iota of truth in it. I'd probably said it to see if I could make you jealous. Rather than take offense, you seemed glad to hear that I'd had some fun. Then, oh surprises of surprises, I went on, implying that I'd buggered the imaginary guy. What did you do then? Nothing less than, right then and there on the strand, get an erection, that mass at your crotch swiftly rigid, straining upward against the pantleg that held it downward. Two passerby caught sight of it, you looked abashed, and I startled.

Halt the action for a moment's reflection. If you want to know the truth—though you don't seem to care to want to know much of anything (except that maybe there's money to be made selling coke, money to liberate you from the boredom you've trapped yourself in—if you care to know something about your old friend Stu, maybe the best buddy a guy ever had, well let me tell you it isn't merely the memory of what we did together which has rekindled my love-obsession at this late date. Instead, it's the thought of how much more we could have done. It wasn't until ten or so years later, after seeing a Jeff Bridges movie, that I was torn by an understanding of what I should have done at that moment in Oceanside when we were twenty-five and thirty, before the sexual revolution, though it was dawning, as we both stared down at the hardon which had so spontaneously sprung. Of course, I should have gotten you to the car, headed home and, while driving, gotten your whanger out, (that vein-gnarled, thick-skinned, glistening buckram) gotten it skinned back, its head flared, ridged and blunt-ended, its deep, shocking-pink, gash-mouth gaping. If it could have spoken it would have simply implored—love me do—however, mute, it was (still is, I hope) a statuesque

TOTEM of you, which I should have given an energetic handjob to along Pacific Coast Highway, El Camino Real, and, unable to take my eyes off the road, unable to get my head down, let your semen fly, figuring there'd be more from where that shot came that night when I should have blown you as long and longer than you cared to be blown, and turned my devotion to the buns a Navy cook had admired and petted, turning you on.

But, mystery of mysteries, true to my stymied form, I didn't grasp the opportunity. Instead I let us waste time, as if time weren't dwindling away, let us squander spontaneity by spending half a balmy evening hitting a few bars in the military town. You got sore because you thought I was ogling the leathernecks, which I suppose I was, but only from the most oblique angle, and only one, with a squared-away face. Was I beginning to fall out of love with you? Or was I afraid of what our love might become? Or afraid of . . . of . . . ?

In any case, by the time we were surrounded by the ferns and philodendrons of our patio, you were out of sorts and, after our customary, hasty coupling, went straight to your room and closed the French doors.

However, there was more to

CUM in our tangled affair, not without wrought heartache.

We agreed to meet the following Friday downtown at a restaurant. You showed up, fifteen or so minutes late, and seeing me, your face filled with pain, then with exasperation, anger, hate, I don't know which. There was a shimmering of tears in your eyes. Without a word you turned and bolted, wanting to get far, far away. Of course I wanted to run after you; I could envision myself wrapping my arms around your legs, crying out as you dragged me down the stairs, "Don't go . . . don't go." As usual, I restrained myself.

Was it less than two hours before you wandered into that bar where we'd met Christmas Eve before last? You sat in a booth across from me, your smile confounded by sadness, and said, "I knew you'd be here."

"I hoped you'd come walking in."

"I took a walk."

"So did I."

"Funny we didn't run into each other."

"Here we are."

"Yeah." Then you added, "There's something I gotta tell you."

"Fire away."

"Have you figured out what it is I don't like about you?"

"I didn't know that you don't like me. I thought you were fond of me."

"You're not listening. Let me ask it like this: have you ever taken the time to figure out what I don't like about this ... about this thing we've got going?"

"Is it because I like sucking your ... ?"

"Not that. I got over that. What drives me batty is that ... that ... goddamn it, you like me too much. When in hell are you going to stop liking me so much?"

You couldn't accuse me of being possessive. I hadn't been. I'd only been there, loving you. And if love isn't the right word, then someone should dream up another. I can't.

"It's stupid the way you go on liking me."

"Why shouldn't I? You're there ... jaunty on the horizon."

You shrugged, as if before a fate it was useless to dodge. We went home wearily, as if having thrashed too long at useless efforts. We bedded down, my head soon in its customary place; you were soon lacing my throat with another issue of Ukrainian seed. After we'd slept soundly, you didn't resist when I, emboldened by late morning's light, aroused you and began working over your crotch and thighs, up one side and down the other. Cautiously, as several laidback marines in the past had said, in more or less the same words: "You can have all my cock and balls you want, but no kissing or licking above the waist." Some had kept on their t-shirts as a barrier separating pelvis and mouth. However most were not adverse to having the hair-ringed, moist, puckered lips of their secret orifice kissed. Your legs spread, allowing my head to get further between them, my tongue strayed closer to—then, all of a sudden, I was on the verge of a climax, rearing back, saying, "Jesus, Nick, I'm coming." And you, out of the marvelous blue, got hold of my hardon, and your hand went wild when the viscous stuff came, and then you were going off, two, four spurts before I got my mouth positioned to get the rest. One might believe that was the true beginning of matrimonial bliss for us. But you withdrew and then spent a very, very long time in the bathroom showering. Later, as we idled at breakfast, you were withdrawn, appearing to contemplate a fate worse than extinction. Or did I imagine that? Was it instead simply a case of *post coitus l'homme est bleu*, that exquisite sadness which comes to lovers. In any case, we remained chaste the following night and all day Sunday in our domesticity, neither saying much. I grew morose with fears I might lose you. Then there was an unexpected call from Vangie, which you refused to take. In fact you bolted from the living room and hurried to the bathroom, where you hid yourself for, how long, a half hour? And, my God, I heard you bawling in there, of all things! My leatherneck husband crying his heart out. I was in agony thinking it was all my fault, realizing how very much our affair was costing you: your pain my doing. When at last you came out, your face puffy and reddened, you glared at me, snapping, "Okay, Markham, I don't want to hear a word about what just happened. Not one word! Not one goddamn question! It's done and forgotten! I don't want that mind of yours trying to analyze it ... do you hear?"

The following Friday evening you didn't show up and the gloom of my quarters was doubled by a heavy downpour outside. The fringes of a tropical storm hit Mexico: it was an excruciating wait from six to eleven, when I began to doze. My sleep was fretful. A shutter banged, and I dared hope you, having misplaced your key, were banging for entrance. At ten next morning, you did arrive, appearing pale and derelict, as if you'd had a bad night on the streets, had gotten drunk, all the more woebegone because of your drenched clothes. You slipped into the bathroom, closed the door. Soon the shower spray was on full force for the longest time, and after the valve was turned off and the room silent, you remained in there long enough for one of Shostakovitch's most somber symphonies to be played on the hi-fi. I worried how heavy your mood would be when you presented yourself to me again. When you did, you'd groomed yourself with great care, put on the snug, beige trousers and the fine polo shirt I'd bought you for Christmas, but you hardly glanced at me. Instead, you went to the sliding glass doors and looked out where ferns and philodendrons pitched in fitful gusts, grunting, saying, "That goddamn wind is going to tear the shit out of my plants."

When I handed you a Bloody Mary, our eyes awry, perhaps each of us fearful as the other to explore our souls, it probably wasn't the best of moments for much scrutiny. You enthroned yourself in your favorite chair, continued to stare at the damage being done on the patio, then grumbled, "It's a fucking humid day. Raunchy as I feel."

"You look splendid."

"Yeah ... yeah ... yeah. What the fuck difference does it make if I look splendid. It's a raunchy world ... right?"

I ventured a question. "Are you about to tell me that I have something to do with your feeling raunchy?"

Your answer was indirect. "You know, sometimes I've wondered what it would be like to be a whore. Did you ever feel like a whore, Markham?" You smiled cruelly and, sitting with your legs spread, opened your fly and brought out the thick, blond member, mocking. Was it self-mockery?

Annoyed, I said, "Were you out selling it last night? You certainly don't sell it here."

Scared of our perverse moods, I fled to the kitchen and fixed us a big brunch. After we'd consumed it and a couple more drinks, I insisted we go to an afternoon movie, to avoid one another yet remain side-by-side in the dark. Later it was my idea that we go down to Tijuana in the continuing rain for old time's sake, to commemorate the other time we were there in a tempest, the night I almost drowned in a riptide, the night each of us tried to fuck the other. Well, this was going to be quite a night too. The two of us had had a lordly portion of booze, watched sailors and marines get rowdy before the Mexican strippers in dives, listened to them hoot and holler for the lazy gals to "take it all off" when, out of the exquisite blue, eternally,

YOU, Nick, leapt onstage, took the spotlight, dropped your drawers to half-mast, pulled up your shirt to bare your waist, did some deep knee bends, got the whanger swinging, then did some butch pelvic grins, inspiring cheers from the audience, then cat calls when you saucily mooned me. Because dark-faced waiters were scowling with menace, you pulled up your pants and we ran out, laughing on the streets, our silence broken, a downpour flushing our faces. How could I not help loving you more and more, since you were determined to be more and more excruciatingly enticing? In the car on the way home, you—as spontaneously as you'd taken center stage—got out of shoes, trousers and shorts, tossed them onto the back seat, rolled down the window letting in the wind and rain. "Feels great," you announced while removing your polo shirt and, buck naked, raised bent knees, placed your feet on the seat, shook your taut member at me, your crewcut sopping, water streaming on your hairless, blond chest in the dashboard's dim gleaming, laughing and saying, "I drive you crazy, don't I?"

Since Babs, lighting up another reefer, seems deeper in a trance than ever, I think unmindful of your endless talk—Since this coke seems to have reduced each of us to an absurd quintessence of himself, perhaps I ought to go ahead and remind you of how you once cut clean to the heart of the matter, how you cut through the malaise of unspoken, unrealized possibilities and thereby got to the asshole of the matter. There you were, grabbing hold of my right hand, removing it from the steering wheel and bringing it not to the upright emblem of your maleness, but lower, below the testes to the dark, deepest recess in the fold of your rump—saying "I've been giving it a lot of thought, Stu, wondering how you like getting your jollies. And all of a sudden I figured out what you like. Am I right? You like to suck them . . . then fuck them." Nick, when you said that your warm, slightly slick anus caved in a bit to the touch of my fingertip. I might have cried out with joy because you'd taken the trouble to give it a "lot of thought", were concerned about how I was going to be more intimately brought off in some consummation of our ragged marriage. On the other hand, I must say I hadn't plotted to bring our affair to this, nor had I in the past required fucking them after sucking them. Which is not to say I hadn't, but only if that's the way events went in bed; which they did sometimes back in the war days when privates, lance corporals and sergeants back from foxholes in Korea on a one-weekend-stand, after being taken care of front side, rolled over and, whether playing possum or not, offered rumps. I'd been to bed with more than enough American men to know the male psyche is more complex than the Good Book says. And, while there are those who live out their lives without letting some psychic layers bloom, there are many—the brawny and tough as well as the effeminate—who know the rectum, too, is a sensual organ and enjoy a good screwing from time to time, though the macho would die before admitting it.

Be that as it may, it was a wonder we didn't have a crackup before I got us home. And then, Nick, there you were (are still in memory) belly down on the sheet, spread-eagled, those two mounds a pale beach sand color in the lighted room, offered without a fidget as I spread them. A line of auburn hair in the hollow of the long cleavage was (is still eternally) exposed. You lifted (lift) your butt, and we placed (place) a pillow under your thighs, your head forever turned to one side on your crossed arms up on another pillow, accepting my kisses on that milk-chocolate-morsel, that tenderest part of you, so sublimely simple after a year and a half of detours, dead ends, the two of us—after your diversions with Bertha and Vangie—back at

GO, beginning again after the flap of confusing signals and that awful bawling of yours in the bathroom (with me thinking I was crucifying you) and then there I was: rimming what was being bestowed, your sphincter dilating, the slick, inner tissue, the far side of your psyche, revealed to the light, an apricot-colored swirl, I letting you know how much I craved you, you pushing it to my lips.

But—or should I say

BUTT, I couldn't go through with it; left it open-ended. There I was, my mouth on the primed prize, and, of all things, what was I repeating forlornly? "Stay as you are ... stay as you are ... stay as you are." A failure which has gnawed at me for the past ten, fifteen years. During that time, I've rationalized it, dissected it, turned it upside-down. But there's no need for me to throw all these weeds of regret, these midunderstandings and neuroses on the table—and you probably wouldn't be much interested at this late day anyway.

Nick, you stayed as you were, whatever you were, and didn't become what you might have become, for better or for worse. You are who you have been, whomever that is. All I know, in the coke's terrible glare, is that you're forty-five, married to a woman neutered by a surgeon's knife after a cancer scare; neutered before you married her so that you were neutered too; so the golden Ukrainian kernel in your father's loins wasn't passed onto the loins of unrealized sons; your father's only son, the Blazhkov line dead. For all that, you might as well have spent a lifetime spilling your seed with yours truly. Or, Narcissus, did you relish being the only cocksman in a house of females all those years, the gals adoring you? We can guess how Babs' second daughter felt. It's no coincidence that the guy who came along, knocked her up then deserted her was an ice-hockey player out of Canada. Judging from the photos I've seen, she fell for him because, as they say, he was a dead-ringer for you. In any case, you are who you are, a once-upon-a-time studsy buddy, now forty-five and adrift in marijuana swamps, discontented with job, home and wife (in fact, next morning, you'll admit you wish she wasn't so fat), and that's the way it goes. But you're not bitter. You are a man with a warm heart, who will honor and obey and never intentionally harm Babs. You helped her raise her daughters, played the man-of-the-house with verve, although her kids have fallen into the errors of the human condition just like the rest of us. I'm sure you'll never turn criminal, only daydream of getting rich selling coke, because you are an honest man who'll stick it out in the boring factory rather than pander to the addiction of others. And we'll never know what you might have become had "the best buddy maybe a guy ever had" that night thoroughly plumbed the core of you. What more can I say?

Does all of the above sound prosaic? Sorry. This lousy drug has failed to fill the house with the wild bouquets needed. Memory does.

We didn't split the blanket immediately thereafter, but had two more bouts: the first when I absurdly thought I could take back what I had declined, actually thought I could force myself on a man who wasn't in the mood. There was quite a wrestling match in bed as I tried to get my pelvis between your legs, you trying to keep my head in its usual place, and when I didn't give up, our grappling grew hectic until the sheets were helter-skelter, the mattress half on and half off the bed frame, the two of us bareassed on the floor. "Okay," you grumbled, "Markham, that's the last time, the last Goddamn time, you hear!" Fearing you might be serious, I let my head drop into its proper place like a water-filled balloon. Another time, you gave me a second chance. Belly down, rump up, the deep seam between those two muscular slabs parted, your bared anus not metaphorical, but literal, explicit, explicitness having much to do with the lure of sex, and already gingerly primed with my lubed finger

BUTT, I couldn't keep myself

up for the fateful insertion, and when this became evident, you snarled, "The trouble with you, Markham, is that you're a limp dick." I'd done it with others and even

YOU the night I'd come in from skinny-dipping in fierce waves—how come not now? Had our year-and-a-half rigamarole, your dalliances with Bertha and Vangie worn me down? Had your crying jag in the bathroom haunted me so—sounding like a soul going to hell—that it wrecked my spontaneity? Or was it that I wanted matters reversed, wanted my marine husband assertive with me, rather than you being the sex object I'd made of you, and you'd let yourself become. It's crossed my mind many times since that I was afraid you'd get to like it and there'd be no stopping you from throwing your fanny all over town. I had reason to think this possible, having encountered hunky guys who couldn't get enough once they'd felt the luxurious slip and slide. One lug of a sergeant out of Texas once confessed, "Next to a good fight, there's nothing I like better than having a big one pumping me." If you were like that I'd lose you for sure. Then there was your line about feeling like a whore! Christ, Blazhkov, another hustler! By then you had become more than a weekend fling, become a whole, palpitating, complex human being, inviolable, your cock the Holy Grail. Or the fault may simply have been in our stars, libido-crossed lovers from the start. In any case, I did not do the deed

AND your return to Bertha hastened our split up. She 'fessed up; her pregnancy was a false alarm. Whad did you do? You went to her Friday evening. What did I do? Sent you packing when you arrived the following morning

AND a year later there was more to come. You were out of the Corps, deciding with whom you'd cast your civilian lot: your new lady friend Babs and her two daughters, or Stu. That's when you came to L.A., where I'd been transferred by the corporation, from where I'd sent you a few letters, *Hail Blazhkov*. That's where you hung around with me a few days, talking about finding a job, of setting up housekeeping together, sharing expenses, saving money for a trip to Europe, although I couldn't say my spirit was in it much. You stayed three or four nights, sleeping on the couch, the two of us tentatively Platonic. Until that last night when we came back at midnight, and your trousers were down as soon as the door was closing, whanger instantly up. In bed, we returned to our beginning, me down on you, you prematurely spurting. Settling after your climax, you asked me in your dulcet baritone, "How was it?" I suspect you hoped my appetite was revived. I was less than enthusiastic. The next day you left. As the poet said, *in my beginning is my end.* Ten years or so later, after seeing a Jeff Bridges movie, I began berating myself for not having steered another course, for not phoning into my office sick that morning, or arranged a vacation, anything to keep us bareassed, to delve further into infatuation, love, lust, whatever, until we wore it out or got beyond it *in a further union, a deeper communion.*

It's still a mystery to me why I didn't. And that mystery, while not a crown of thorns, has been a prickly bouquet.

THREE

Babs apparently realizes that the coke, rather than set us into flight, has made us zombies, ghostly in the hard light, showing our age. She has nothing to fear for the moment, and so shuffles off to bed, leaving us alone to continue our disjunctive monologues. I haven't the faintest idea what I just said in a long, complex sentence and am weary of trying to be grammatical while I go on avoiding the issue. Maybe it's time to be silent, to simply say goodbye, farewell, *Sayonara,* then be still,

but still moving,

or do I get up from my chair and, against inertia, will myself to cross over memory's flowers, strewn on the floor, cross over at last to

YOU and put my arms around your neck and kiss your brow. I do this before going to my grave in commemoration of how we were at twenty-five and thirty. I smile, laugh softly in the night's hush, say "Do you know—in a way, our love was as ill-fated as Scarlett and Rhett's?"

You stop talking: your chalky face slightly startled. You don't brush me away, yet you want me to withdraw. I do, for a moment. But so there's no mistake, I kiss you again, this time on your neck and say, "If you can remember anything, Nick ... remember one thing when you're bones in a coffin—in my soul's eyes you will always look exactly as you did that night you first stripped for me. Remember? I'd come in from skinny-dipping and there you were in a lighted bedroom stark naked . . . the sight of you a bolt of lightning . . . and what we did was thunder and lightning."

There, it's been said

ALOUD. Silence, withered blooms, and dead men follow my avowal.

I kiss your throat again
My hands move down on your arms,
I'm hoping to get your pants down one more time,
But you push me away.

≠

Well, that should have been the end of it, forever. However there is always morning-after mopping up to be done. The papers on the car's sale have to be signed. You sleep late, Babs and I take care of the transaction. The next train won't be until one in the afternoon, so I have a three-hour wait. I could leave my cab and kill time in the Baths, but at this hour the stragglers will be screwed-out. Why bother? Frankly, I don't want to see you again and hope you sleep through my departure, sleep the rest of your life away, for that matter. Not that I'm angry because you rejected my advances last night. That's understandable; any man has the right not to be in the mood all the time. What galls me is that when you were ready, you toddled off to bed, leaving me sitting in a hard chair in the dinette with that naked light bulb hanging over my head, leaving me with my head tilted forward like a man who'd been shot. It was Babs who had the decency to come shake my shoulders, and show me to the guest room. Really, Nick, as a host you've become a dolt.

However, Bab's tells me the plan is that we'll go to our favorite Mexican restaurant for *machaca*. Once you're up and ready, your wife, at the last moment, decides she won't join us. I suppose so we can have final words alone together. No doubt Babs knows she has nothing to fear now. I'll bet she pours herself a glass of wine after we exit.

And we do have final words, an argument snapping as we sit on the veranda overlooking the bay marina. It appears neither of us cares to break the funk we're obviously fixed in. The scene around us isn't very peppy either. Maybe it's the aftereffects of coke, but the water seems flat, leadened, the air dead, or we're dead to its touch. The sky seems tattletale gray instead of morning blue, and, though white canvas is raised to the wind, the sailboats seem stalled, and, my God, why aren't the seagulls flying? They perch at the edges of roofs stymied. A few waddle this way and that in a malaise of crankiness. Only one stretches its wings as if about to take off, to soar, but gives up and settles back into doldrums.

We sit at a table under a pink-and-white striped umbrella. Without love in my heart I say, "Frankly, Nick, I think coke sucks."

Not a trace of friendliness in your reply, "It was a rotten trip," you grunt. "I guess it depends on who you snort with."

"I guess." Then a stray question occurs. "Would Mozart have Mozarted ... would Ravel have Raveled if they'd been saturated with coke? Wouldn't their spirit atrophy?"

"What in hell's that got to do with it?"

"Perhaps nothing, perhaps a lot."

"You know, there's something I always wondered about you ... just what did you see in all that classical stuff? Maybe you were a little bit phony. Let me tell you, Stu, the world would be the same place if Mozart and that other guy had never existed."

"I take it you don't believe in the refinements of civilization?"

Your face ugly with stubbornness: "No."

"Well, I do. I believe the hearts and minds of us all—even you—have been enhanced by those refinements. Without them, we might as well be baboons compulsively eating bananas, swinging in trees."

"What's wrong with that?"

"Being baboons?"

"Yeah."

"I suppose it takes all kinds ... You can have your coke, your bananas and your trees. I'll take Mozart and ....," with a flourish I add, "... cock."

To our surprise, your young friend, John is standing before us along with his gal. He'd called wanting to talk to you, and Babs told him where you could be found. We are introduced. He's a lithe, rangy fellow in mod clothes, his hair wavy black, his face smooth, pale flesh, sporting a trim mustache and faintly rosy cheeks. His smiling eyes are impertinent as he looks me up and down, sure of himself and the chick draped at his side. She is pretty, well-attired, ringlets cascading around her beaming face, but for the moment she is deferring to him. He's twenty-five or so, prematurely rich you've said, full of good humor as he takes a seat like a prince. The waitress, eyes on him, fawns some as she takes the order for two *Ramos Fizzes*.

An ebullient conversation begins between you two. I barely listen; for all I care, you may today enter a life of crime and luxury with his ilk. As for me, in exactly ten minutes I'm getting my bag out of your car, catching a taxi and getting to the depot, out of here.

The times comes. I rise and make a small excuse. You appear surprised but don't try to detain me. Not too long after I'm seated in a drab Amtrak club car, as glittering San Diego slips out of past, present and future on fixed rails below. I remember something a friend once said, the same one who told me to kick you out when you were putting it to Bertha. His second piece of advice, when he saw I was letting you slip away: "If you let him go back to being heterosexual, he'll botch up his life. Wait and see."

I'd never believed him before but, now, after your complaints last night, I wonder ... I wonder. But enough is enough. I open my *The New York Review of Books* and read Susan Sontag on photography. Taking what may be my last view of the beach near San Clemente while humming the long, lovely melody from Ravel's G Minor Concerto, I skim the photograph album kept in the privacy of my skull: shots of marines, naked with hardons, long and short, snakey and hunky, balls and all, and not merely two dozen red cocky blooms. I smile and think, "Nick, you stayed on a while and I might pine for you more, but I have to keep moving, moving on to tumultuous, tempestuous Manhattan, Hong Kong on the Hudson, there to build an office and staff, to deliver a product, for better or for worse, in competition-run-amuck,

AND, before I know it I'm there, dodging throngs on sidewalks, my eyes straying to hundreds upon hundreds of NYC workmen, telephone linemen, sweaty carpenters, hairy-chested stonemasons and gritty demolition crews, the brawny guys who endlessly toil to keep the big, bad monolith of a city from falling further into chaos. My libido is inclined to flirt with the best-looking, particularly the Italians. However, wearing a Walkman head-set and listening to the crisp sound of Mozart's *The Hunt* quartet, I chasten my glances while walking to and from the office. I don't cruise more than one or two in the horny fraternity on my way to the Met. This afternoon they are performing *Pelleas et Melisande*.

Wonder what life will be like at sixty?

BLOCK'S SPARTANS

This piece is dedicated to all the boys in uniform
who did . . .

ONE

With slow, circular motions, having greased and massaged it, Colonel Block without haste slipped a finger from Corporal Riley's rectum, and the warm sphincter gripped tight on the draw. More lubricant was applied, and the finger was reinserted by stages, the top of it causing the chocolate-hued anus to cave in, the first knuckle parting it wider. Then half the finger was enfolded, the second knuckle circled by glistening, chestnut-colored hair. During this priming, the naked corporal remained on a desktop, flat on his broad back, his bent knees draw toward hair covered, dense pectorals, his hefty buttocks bowed at the wood surface's edge, the cleavage down the center darkly hairy, spread like an offering. Standing nearby, stripped too, built like a robust peasant, Sergeant Kinsbursky watched with eagerness in his blue eyes, pumping on himself, saying, "Shit, sir, if you don't let me into that beautiful asshole pretty soon, I'm going to go off ... let it fly and waste it." Block gestured for him to come closer and, after greasing the sergeant's chunky cock, looked to where its flared, peach colored head plugged the orifice, his fingertips touching where the men were joined, feeling the shaft glide in.

Three evenings before, after his unit's first trek through the desert, the officer had singled out the rangy, plainfaced Riley to come to his quarters. The door was closed, and they stood face to face, alone, still partially dazed by the day's long exertions, their dusty, khaki uniforms sweat-stained, Riley at attention, although Block had said, "At ease." What the colonel meant to say next was something he had never said to any man serving for or with him, though recently he'd wanted to say it to any number of strapping corporals, sergeants and lieutenants. When spoken, his words would defy tradition, undermine the Academy's code and, in normal circumstances, would negate his right to command men. However, nothing was the same; grave errors had been made worldwide; the planet was half wrecked by prolonged war; the mission his twenty volunteers had accepted would prove to be his and their last—of that he was convinced. On the other hand, there were unchangeables, and one of these was the enduring maleness of men like Riley; brave, of sound physique, restive in spite of the seasoning of discipline, and, of course, in need of an orgasm. In light of that, the eight words Block chose were: "Corporal ... let's have a look at your cock."

The odors of desert brush and dust mingled with that of human perspiration. Without looking down, the colonel undid the brass buckle at the soldier's waist, musing, a simple enough thing to do, yet it might be an invitation to a brusque, contemptuous rejection. While considering thin, orange flecks in the otherwise brown irises of the corporal's eyes, Block lowered the zipper. Riley was twenty-eight, in the army seven years, a silent man, once a sergeant but busted three years before following a barracks brawl. While considering dirtcaked sprouts of hair in the nostrils immediately before him, the officer proceeded, unsnapping the drawers' buttons, parting the cloth, feeling a thickness of coarse crotch hair. Riley was from Wyoming; widowed, had lost his wife and children in an air raid; a tested warrior. He'd volunteered for the mission, his reason barked out in eight words at first muster, "To get back at the rotten enemy, sir." Without looking down, Block cupped a palm to get the heft of testicles, which, in contrast to the room's heat, seemed cool, Riley's squarish, whisker-stubbled, tanned face tense. The man was six-foot-two, one-hundred-and-ninety pounds, a solid loner respected by his peers. Big and heavy balls, Block meditated. Gazing at the crew-cut hair, auburn under a fine coating of desert grit, the commissioned officer opened the non com's shirt and, while window panes rattled from blasts of wind, moved the garb off meaty shoulders, and, when the sleeves were drawn down dangling arms, Riley's right bicep jerked in two quick spasms. Dark hair beneath his t-shirt showed through, and two round, brown teats, delineated by clinging damp cloth, the man's musculature making him appear somewhat brutish. But Riley was no dumbbell; his file read an IQ of a hundred-and-forty; a laconic, sometimes taciturn, underachiever, who no doubt accepted his fate for what it was without carping. His undershirt raised halfway, his britches and shorts spread in a wide V, the man was bared from rib cage to crotch, abdomen flat, swirls of hair over rippled belly muscles. He stood no longer precisely at attention but then not at ease either, as the colonel looked down to the knobby, circumcised head of his puckered cock and asked calmly, "How long has it been since you've had sex?"

After his Adam's Apple made two gulping movements, the corporal answered in a thick voice, "Quite a while, sir."

"Aren't the women in our war-torn world putting out?"

"I suppose ... if a guy goes looking."

"Haven't you been looking?"

"Not lately."

"No doubt you mourn your wife and children."

"Yes."

"It's a mournful world we've made."

There was no answer to that.

"Yet there is still desire. You must guess by now that I plan on giving you some head." Block fondled the limp member, which began to emerge from the mat of hair. "In spite of your mourning, I'm sure you still get a hardon from time to time."

"Yes."

"Do you encourage it, as I do now?" The cock continued to elongate and soon was firm enough for Block to squeeze a handful. After several moments, he let it go to consider the whole cylindrical mass standing at a ninety-degree angle from the pelvis, its covering membrane brownish-pink, a network of raised veins beneath, the compact inner bulk stretching higher. Block suddenly squatted before it. An excellent, classical cock, he thought, smelling and tasting it, as a tense muscle on Riley's right leg winced.

The corporal's baritone voice asked, "You sure you want to go through with this, sir?"

"Very sure." At that moment, the colonel wanted to yank the trousers down, draw Riley to the floor and get to the task, however he also wanted the man to finish undressing himself, in acceptance of what they were about to share, wanted it to be with comingled intentions. So Block backed away, stood, picked up the fallen shirt, hung it on the back of a chair and then crossed the room to a small table, upon which a bottle of bourbon, three glasses, and a pitcher of water stood.

"You're in officer territory now ... so you can have a drink ... no ice or mix though ... just hootch with water." Against the sound of the wind hard upon frail walls, he added, "Of course ... since I've just broken the rules, you'd be in your rights to zip up, tell me to go to hell and clear out." Without turning to see what Riley was or wasn't doing, he poured the amber liquid into a glass, about a double shot, diluted it and asked, "Have you ever wondered why officers are allowed to drink on base and not enlisted men?" There was no answer. "It's because we're supposedly gentlemen ... at least, made so by an act of Congress. It's believed we can handle the stuff, although, as everyone knows, some of my commissioned brothers get shit-faced regularly, as the expression goes ... and make donkeys of themselves. But, if the law says we're gentlemen, then, by almighty God ... who probably doesn't exist ... we *are* gentlemen ... to the death.

The afternoon's heat was trapped in the room, and sweat continued to break on Block's brow; tricklets of it ran down his lean neck. He glanced at the cumbersome air-conditioner set in a wall, but rather than turn it on, after pouring a second drink, he crossed to a window and slid its lower half up, then did the same at another, letting the wind in. He gazed out at a deserted compound and swirling dust, a row of dilapidated barracks of sun-dried wood, then, straight ahead, into a bronze dusk which silhouetted distant, jagged peaks in a wasteland. Before returning to Riley with the drinks, he removed his boots and clothes at the window, letting blasts of hot air evaporate sweat on his taut, smooth-skinned body and buffet his pubic hair. He pulled down the faded orange, rolldown shades, which caught eccentric gusts, lifting, fluttering, falling, lifting again, making a faint crackling. Stroking his erection and considering the sweep of desert, he mused, man and desolation ... man and the hostile universe we find ourselves in ... man and the war we make. A sad smile came to his chapped, coral-hued lips. Aloud he said, "In spite of it all, we remain ardent."

Standing before the corporal again, he lifted a glass in toast. "Here's to you and your fine cock." It had lost its former stiffness but only some of its length, drooping over a bulging scrotum. With two wetted fingers, Block anointed it, staring straight into Riley's eyes, which instantly averted. "Don't look away. I know you've been trained not to look too closely into an officer's eyes ... not to question his inner thoughts and possible madness ... but, my splendid chap, you did nothing to cover up while I was getting our booze. You've remained available ... at parade rest ... knowing you've got nothing to be ashamed of. And look ... with a little coaxing it's coming up again ... metaphorically, a soldier standing up to its duty. So accept my eyes. Since you're admirably hung, I would venture to say this isn't the first time someone has wanted to blow you ... and I mean another man, perhaps even an officer."

Two pairs of eyes, one set brown and the other blue, searched, and after swallowing more of his drink, the muscles of his swarthy neck flexing, Riley replied, "A sergeant once, sir."

"How did that come about?"

There was obvious reluctance to speak of it, so Block led the way, "A sergeant had his eyes on you, and ..."

"I was a young recruit."

"Nothing unusual about that. I'd say sergeants have had their eyes on young recruits since man first began gathering armies. And this sergeant approached you, right?"

"One day he told me to follow him into a deserted warehouse ... and in there told me to drop my drawers because he was going to ... to ... suck my dick."

"That bluntly?"

"He said that if I blabbed about it afterward he'd make my life miserable."

"So you let him?"

There was a nod.

"Did you enjoy it?"

"No complaint."

"And of course he liked it."

"Well, he wanted to do it ...," Riley cut the sentence off.

" ... wanted to do it a second time, no doubt."

"We were stationed in the boondocks ... as remote as this place here ... and ..."

" ... there were no women, and you were frequently hard-up."

"I couldn't figure what he got out of it, but it didn't take long, and there were other guys going into that warehouse."

"To the lucky sergeant?"

"No. There were others who liked doing it. One night there were ...," the corporal once again broke off.

"Come, come, Riley. The world has gone to hell, so why should we two grown men hesitate to discuss man's nature, for better or worse? You were about to say ..."

"There were six or seven studs in there in the dark having their jollies. Things got pretty wild ... asshole wild. I didn't know men could get like that."

"Are you telling me you favored the sergeant with a buggering?"

"Yeah."

"Your cock appears to have fond memories of it. It's come to attention, harder than the proverbial rock." Block criss-crossed their erections, one larger and darker than the other, both equally rigid. "So you've been initiated." He lifted the glass again. "Here's to the blow-job you're about to get . . . in honor of all honest men." With an agile movement he squatted before the crotch and drew the thick cockhead into his mouth and began to engulf the shaft, which tasted salty, gamey, bourbonish. His salivary glands wet the mouthful, Block's lips gliding further along the mass, the bulged, central tube firm against the sensitive skin of his lower lip. He went back and forth methodically, back and forth, withdrawing from time to time to lick, to rub the cock over his face and to suck the man's testicles, feeling as if he were taking a sacrament. His mate's thighs began to make slow, undulating movements. Riley pushed his member deeper, and the colonel's throat, rather than resist, made swallowing motions, a thought in the officer's mind: I blow this earnest fellow, therefore I am. I herald this lonely soldier, therefore he is.

After a while, the corporal said, "Jesus, sir . . . if you keep that up, I'm going to come."

Disengaging himself, the colonel replied, "I suppose there'll be more. We have the night. Or are you the kind who, once he's unloaded, bolts?" There was no need to rush, so he arose, saying, "If we're going to do this up right, shouldn't you get bareassed? As a matter of fact, let's have a look at your butt, too."

Riley tossed off his t-shirt, raised a foot to a chair and began hurriedly unlacing a boot. After removing both, he stepped free of his pants and shorts, asking, "Shouldn't we lock the door and back away from the windows, sir?"

"Why? No one will come or look in. If someone does, why should we object?" Block was about to add that he planned on blowing all twenty of the men who had volunteered for the bloody mission and that he planned, before the hour of their death, to encourage these brawny soldiers to a last, great sexual release on earth. However, it was best not to speak of plans. For the moment, it was enough that Riley was naked and waiting for him a short distance removed. Before going to him, the officer laid out his trousers on the desktop, aligned their pantlegs and did the same to the corporal's. Then the two soldiers stood face-to-face, looking each other up and down; one frame powerful; the other trim. For a moment, it seemed they might embrace, except for an almost bashful hesitancy in the younger. Block urged his partner to sit on the cot against the wall. When Riley did, the big-limbed fellow took the classic position, by instinct spreading his legs, moving his pelvis forward to the bed's edge and reclining his shoulders against the wall, his full length available to his seducer. The corporal swiped sweat from beneath his scrotum, causing his hardon to lurch this way and that over his naval, which was circled with sable-colored hair. Block took the devotional position, kneeling. He lifted the fellow's substantial legs and placed each on a shoulder, so they were bent at the knees, Riley's feet dangling at the small of the officer's back, Block's head at the spread pelvis, the purely animal part of the man, blood beating in a reddened cock, egg-shaped testicles bulging in a tight, wrinkled sack of skin, hair wet with perspiration, the cock root bulging above the tender, hairy hollow on the underside of the butt, the colonel's face positioned to feast. His mouth gaped and soon was filled with scrotum, Block musing, I suck his nuts, therefore I am—he sighs, therefore he is. Then he placed his tongue's tip into the hair at the warm anus, his nostrils inhaling. After kissing the orifice, his voice was heard murmuring, "Lyons . . . Lyons."

≠

Block had chosen Riley from his twenty volunteers first because the corporal resembled the leatherneck who had initiated him six years before. At that time, divorced seven months and on leave in the States recuperating from a wound, Block had met the marine sergeant in an elevator of a second-rate, Manhattan hotel. The unhandsome jarhead, after a perfunctory salute, had looked the officer up and down, circumspectly at first, then with brazen intent and a wry grin, hand in pocket making adjusting motions at his crotch. Block instantly felt a jolt in his loins, an affirmation entirely unexpected. He had been impotent more than three months, since taking a piece of shrapnel, since lying among wounded men on the floor of a helicopter, from time to time delirious, imagining himself in a tangle of severed legs, arms and heads, the chop-chop-chopping of the aircraft reverberating in his ears, aching in his skull, blood all over him, his blood and that of comrades. He had tried to get up, wanted to be on his feet in defiance of his stricken state, but a hard, unseen force kept him pinned. He flailed against it, needing to assert himself, to keep death at bay. He didn't remember when, but amidst fragmentary feeling and consciousness he suddenly had a desire to masturbate and, hearing senseless laughter, perhaps his own, perhaps not, he imagined himself ripping open his trousers, but, rather than finding what he sought, he came upon a hole in his groin, a hole deep enough to engulf a fist. He didn't panic, instead felt only keen curiosity, remembering fellow officers saying he was a rare bird, able to distill his emotions to an essence, to get a fix on them, a stranglehold. Moments or hours later in non sequiter, he was recalling the names of battles he'd studied at the Academy: Marathon and the Somme, Agincourt and Antietem; men in tactics and countertactics, rushing to slaughter. Nights later, no telling how many, he drifted back and forth between sleep and wracked wakefulness, heard the chop-chop-chopping, wanted to jack off, felt for his cock but found that gaping hole, saw himself pulling out inches of intestines, considering them curiously—Salamis and Waterloo, Balaclava and Iwo Jima. Mind seemingly separated from body, he saw himself stretched on an operating table, whole again, damn glad to have an erection, which a nurse, smiling exquisitely, fondled dulcetly commenting, "It's a nice one, major." However, a masked surgeon intruded with a raised scalpel, which he swiftly wielded, and red liquid shot up like irregular jets of semen in orgasm. Chop-chop, chop-chop.

Then he was just from a bath and laid back in the bedroom of his civilian home, or it could have been the honeymoon suite of a French Riviera hotel, his wife Kim giving him a blowjob. While courting, he'd often observed that she was the classiest of gals, elegant, from good family and finishing school, into culture and the arts—she coming and going, quoting Emily Dickinson, Yeats and e e cummings. So it was a surprise when she so willfully went down on him, having uncinched the towel around his waist, looking him up and down quoting something from Whitman about the body electric, merriment in her hazel eyes as she led him to the bed, upon which they'd coupled an hour before. While he'd showered, she had brushed her hair and applied fresh makeup, so, lowering his eyes, he gazed at the glistening, crimson lips kissing the pale rose head of his cock. Once the sucking began, she barely let up, her groom puzzled by her need to do this, her determination, which didn't diminish during the seven years of their marriage. On occasion he returned the gesture in sixty-nine, however his cunnilingus was, at best, an exercise, while her fellatio was avid. And it was not any lessening of infatuation with his body which caused Kim to seek a divorce.

Dearest, dearest Tom, Last week when you were here, so, so near, I nearly told you what I must write now—what I've shamefully needed to tell you more than a year—have not been able to speak of to that cool, cool handsome face of yours, because, as you know, I fall in love again and again, as if for the first time, everytime you stand before me. The sight of your virile, tantalizing body makes me delirious. Everyone knows it. It could go on eternally. But, I must cry halt. Not because I have had enough of you. I will never have that—which is the torment. Tom, you must know your wife is wretchedly lonely week after week, month after month, when you are not here reminding her in the flesh of her love. She can't—won't!—ask you to desert your cherished career to be at her side, though she aches to the core of her womb for that. But it is hopeless unless you will be my daily husband. Tom, my cry is this—your Kim must be free to have a husband who will be with her week after week—weeks and months of nights. She must have an ordinary husband who does not regularly risk never returning—a husband who doesn't regularly risk death. Oh, God, how we admire that cool bravery in you, yet it is this reckless bravery which, in your absences, torments the woman who..."

Truth was, Kim had already chosen a new mate, and this was a dear John letter, which the then Major Block read over and over until the meaning was gone out of it, until he saw nothing but black marks on paper. The divorce proceedings were completed without fuss, but, five months later, while recuperating from surgery, he had a recurring dream of Kim coming to him, talking her highbrow chatter, "Like the women who come and go talking of Michelangelo" in Eliot's poem; talking of Gauguin and Jackson Pollack while she played with his cock, getting it up, pausing to kiss it, at last speechlessly going down, the convalescent wondering if these dreams were his fight against the lingering impotency. The dreams disappointed however, for each time he felt on the verge of a climax, there was the chop-chop-chopping, and he was cockless, and Kim reared back from the hole at his crotch with blood on her face.

Nonetheless, he kept his cool. In fact, out of the muddle, something new was emerging in these hallucinations, something which intrigued him. In one, then another, after a mixup of images, tall Sergeant Lyons, who had been captured and killed by the enemy, walked into the bedroom, disrobed piece by piece slowly until he was brawny naked and, with little ado, stretched out on the bed and let the woman begin savoring his flesh, while Block gazed at the two, feeling no particular emotion, instead heightened curiosity. Lyons' head dangled lifelessly to one side, and his prone torso and limbs were as pale as a cadaver's, so he seemed dead, except for his jutting erection.

Someone had said, "They sure killed that poor son-of-a-bitch." The enemy has sliced and burnt his skin. His head had been hacked off and placed on a stake. Another stake had been driven up his ass, the blood-drained corpse set on a road alongside the head. Block and his men came upon the awful sight, stopped in their tracks and stared at the sergeant's remains in stupefaction. "Jesus Christ. Couldn't they have just killed him. Did they have to do all that?" Block remained silent, feeling as if he'd been struck by a mallet, for Lyons had been the first man he'd had a special regard for. It wasn't just that Lyons had been a tough soldier and a skilled sergeant, a man who had kept things to himself and had had little to say except when making sure the men serving him knew what they were supposed to be doing and not letting up on them until they did it right. He'd been attached to Block only two months and had proved himself to be better than his reputation, but it was more than that which had kindled Block's high regard for him. The usually aloof officer had found himself thinking about this man altogether too often and too intently. Once seeing Lyons bathing in a lagoon, he had been stunned by his maleness; tall, stacked, hairy and hung. Then the terrible day had come when he'd seen how Lyons had been tortured; flesh seared, bamboo slivers driven through his eyes, cheeks and neck, through his testicles and cock, too. Had the man been conscious when all this had been done to him? The question itself threw Block into a gloom which had possessed him for days, and it was unlike him to be unable to look away from butchery, to keep a clear head, and to do what had to be done next in the course of warfare. The morbidity which had beleaguered him was probably the cause of that mission's failure—might explain fully why he'd blundered and let his unit be ambushed, why he'd lost more of his men and gotten wounded himself, to end up on the floor of a helicopter along with a few miserable survivors; a chop-chop-chopping throbbing in his ears.

In his hospital bed, he dreamed of Kim licking the length of Lyon's cock, which seemed to have become larger. Block felt no particular emotion, though his right hand did move to his own crotch, and he wanted to masturbate hard while he watched the sergeant get sucked, "Except I kept finding this gushy hole," he said to a civilian therapist he visited after being released from medical confinement. He sought consultation on his impotency and erotic dreams, and the elderly doctor let him ramble. "It was funny how she ... everytime she came up for a deep breath ... started talking about Motherwell or Chagall, the painters ... or quoting Auden ... with witty asides, sounding like Katherine Hepburn ... looking gorgeous, by the way ... her skin and eyes aglow ... almost iridescent ... a vital, happy woman doing two of the things she liked doing best ... chit-chatting elegantly and sucking cock."

When the silver-haired psychologist questioned him on his feelings for Lyons, Block didn't come immediately to the point. "I've lived with men in close quarters much of my life, eating, drinking, drilling, bathing, sleeping...and fighting alongside them ... and never felt anything but pride to be with the best of them, but contempt for fools and cowards. Many are fools, and there are more cowards than anyone cares to admit. But then there are a lot of heroes. By that I don't mean swashbucklers. I mean the kind of man who stands up to adversity—a bad turn of events—who keeps his head straight and his mouth shut, who, without squirming and complaining, does what needs to be done, no matter how dangerous, and sticks it out to the end—even if it means his skin."

"And Lyons was one of these?"

"Yes."

"But you felt more than that for him, I gather."

"That's the point."

"Can you describe your feelings?"

"Probably not."

"When did you first realize you felt more than ... than respect?"

"Right off."

In Florida, it was pouring summer rain when Lyons had come to report for his new assignment. The sergeant had not made a dash through the wet weather, instead headed across the compound to an office building at an untroubled gait, Block observing through the window. Minutes later, Lyons was standing at attention on the other side of a desk, having made a quick, sure salute, his drenched khaki clinging to the frame nature had given him. The file on him was impressive enough, but he was also an exceptional physical specimen. It wasn't just that he was six-foot-two, with broad shoulders and big hands. The way he held his crew-cut head indicated alertness. His muscular neck indicated a tempered forcefulness. And there was more. Block later described him as an easygoing powerhouse.

"And he looked at me without any complications ... instead a straightforward, silent questioning."

"Questioning of what?" the doctor asked.

"To see what kind of man I was."

"Did he?"

"I think he sized me up in a few minutes ... enough to know we could work together."

"Did you take a quick liking to one another?"

"Respect."

Block, however, didn't confide what had strayed to mind when he observed the way Lyons' sopped trousers caressed a bulge at his pelvis, didn't tell of his quick, unformed speculation on what the man's sex life might be like. The young officer was surprised by it. He'd never considered this of another man; it was none of his business. Yes, every soldier had a sex life, whether it be active, repressed or something in between, but that was engaged in off base and had nothing to do with soldiering. Block believed a man could perform his duties well whether he was a womanizer or a Puritan. Nonetheless, seeing Lyons for the first time, he found himself instantly convinced that the strapping man was a potent stud and found himself hoping Lyons was being well taken care of.

Their subsequent preparations for a mission in a war-fomented world soon preoccupied them. Any sexuality was kept at bay. that is, until a month later, on the other side of the planet, at the site of a tropical lagoon when Block had the occasion to observe Lyons bathing naked, when he saw how superb the body was and how nobly this man was endowed. Some distance from the watering hole, Block stopped short and would never know how long he stood gazing at Lyons, who stood out from the pack of six or so other nude forms. He became flustered and saw that Lyons, perhaps knowing he had been singled out, removed himself further from his comrades and stood full-front with water halfway between his knees and crotch. Some parrots cawed overhead. A humid breeze rustled the foliage. Shifting rays of light glinted on wet leaves and the lagoon's surface. Time seemed suspended, and Lyons, as if beckoning his admirer to do the same, looked down to where he pulled back his foreskin and then lathered his cockhead, taking his time at it, giving himself a lift, doing it without any impertinence or taunting, but matter-of-factly as if he were alone in a shower, a self-assured man at the ritual of bathing, reminding himself of his cherished gender. The officer blushed for the first time in years, but it was long moments before the burn broke his trance. He turned quickly away, presumably to go about his business, but, once hidden in a copse steaming with heat and a recent rain, he returned his eyes to where the sergeant lifted handfuls of water and let it fall over his head, the liquid slithering over his rough face; in its descent over a raised neck tendon, wet hair clinging to the contours of his pectorals, his chest like a bronze breastplate—altogether statuesque, but not a statue of a trim athlete; like myself, the major thought; instead a statue sculpted in honor of brute brawn. No dainty, little Grecian penis on him either. Lyons was hung—hung.

While the two of them, Block and the therapist, sat in white, cushioned chairs, surrounded by yellow blooming acacia in a rarified afternoon light, they were joined by two young nudes, male and female. She, buxom in spite of her slight frame, stood before Block, making herself available for him to feel if he cared to do so, her firm, tanned, round brown-nippled breasts inches from his face while she undid the buttons of his shirt. He guessed it was a first step in his therapy. His belt buckle was parted, his fly gradually unzipped, the catches of his shorts unsnapped one by one, his abdomen and flaccid genitals bared. He felt quite foolish, although the touch of her smooth tits, then their smell when she pressed them to his face, was pleasurable enough. However he got nothing of a rise, not even when she knelt between his spread legs and began fellatio on him. Watching her, the dreams of Kim blowing Lyons became uppermost, and then he recalled an exchange between the sergeant and himself the day before he came upon the man bathing.

It had been just before sunset in pouring rain, a torrid squall drenching the already sodden terrain. Block's men were struggling with a truck stuck in mud, pushing at the obstinate vehicle's weight, up to their knees in muck. Suddenly, irate with the prolonged storm, the sludge, the unyielding mass, Sergeant Lyons had blurted, "Cocksucker! Goddamn cocksucker!" Under the circumstances, it was not an unusual thing to say. Men used the phrase time and again, in frustration, anger, with embellishments, "Mother-fucking cocksucker ... cock sucking assholes." The words seemed inexplicably to give them great satisfaction. Block rarely used the obscenity, and then only under his breath, but, for reasons he had no time to understand, he was pleased that Lyons had just spoken it with such gusto. However, by the change of expression on Lyons' face, it was clear he regretted cussing, perhaps because he felt it improper before an officer, particularly one of such impeccable bearing. After steadying his breath from huffing and puffing, he added, "Sorry, sir." It was a genuine apology, all the more honest because of the man's square, weathered, rain-flushed face.

"No need ... no need to ... apologize," Block replied. Nothing more had been said. They returned to their task, mutually straining against the bulk, muscles flexing hard, and, after the truck had at last been budged, rocked and rolled free, the two men, released from exertion, quivering, smiles coming to their faces, considered one another, as though they had just shared an intimacy. Block's gaze took in the nakedness of Lyons' shoulders, the rich brown hair of his solid chest, the flatness of his square belly, also, again, the soaked trousers clinging to thighs and sturdy legs. After Lyons turned away, freeing his right leg from the mud, his buttocks too were delineated, wet cloth deep in the center crack between the two bunched mounds, a great rump, the officer mused, and days later would add, a rump the filthy enemy shoved a sharp stake up after torturing him. Bamboo needles had been stuck through Lyons' cheeks, eyes, scrotum and cock. Someone seeing this said in horror, "They sure killed that poor son-of-a-bitch." Later someone else muttered, "The rotten cocksuckers who did that oughta be skinned and roasted alive." The officer had replied, "Try to forget it ... try ..." However he had not and more than once it brought tears to his eyes.

On the lawned grounds of an estate where Block had gone in hopes of getting over his impotency, he looked to where the naked, young woman, sitting on his lap, rubbed his withered member back and forth against the hair puff covering her vulva, the smooth flesh of her soft butt on his legs, she amorously considering him, yet without guile. She separated the labials, but the touch of slightly moist, slightly purplish tissue against his pale penis did nothing to enliven him. He looked two yards away where the psychologist was blowing the young man. The willowy youth stood tall with hands on his hips, calmly gazing down at the silvery top of the head which moved back and forth. The elderly man's cheeks were drawn deeply in, and, judging from the slurping, the engaged mouth was maintaining considerable suction.

After awhile, the doctor withdrew from the crotch, looked at Block and said, "I gather from a certain tone in your voice that you never quite approved of your wife enjoying fellatio as much as she did ... or at least that you never quite understood it."

"It was always kind of a mystery to me. I'm pretty good at plowing a woman and hanging in there until she has her orgasm. We did a lot of that, so it kind of puzzled me why she was so keen on doing that afterwards. Sometimes it would take half an hour to work up another climax for her."

"A question occurs. Were you by and large faithful to her when you were married?"

"Completely. When I was at my job there was no sex at all, not even if I was assigned to a place where women were available. When I got home, she and I hit the sack plenty."

"And you could compartmentalize it that neatly?"

"Yes," Block answered looking to where the doctor stroked the young man's erection and kept it up.

"How about before you were married? Did you have much sex then?"

"There wasn't much time for it. But now and then, with the right woman, there was plenty . . . but a soldier's better off not thinking about it too much."

"So you've been chaste most of your life . . . or at least for considerable periods of your life?"

"Yes."

"Did you masturbate much?"

"I haven't done that since I was a stupid kid . . . since before I went into the Academy. You have to quit it then."

The young woman had ceased making over Block, who, feeling even more foolish, sat with his trousers and shorts around his ankles, his male member shriveled. On the other hand, the therapist had a hardon and had lifted his long, white robe to bare it. Presently, the lass was kneeling between his legs, her hair spread over his thighs, her head beginning to bob. The man again sucked on the standing youth, later to disengage and say, "Once you get a taste for fellatio, it's very tantilizing and ultimately satisfying. Has it never once crossed your mind that you might, at least try to, suck a cock?"

"I suppose it's crossed my mind but I've never made a

move to do anything about it."

"Have you ever let a man suck yours?"

"Not a man . . . a high school friend. We were on a hunting trip in the mountains, just the two of us. I was a pretty cocky athlete. I had a notion of what he wanted. I figured that by the way he looked at me in the showers. But I didn't know exactly what he wanted. I think I was interested in finding out."

Young Tom even egged his friend on. They'd been in deep woods, and Tom had had to urinate and had made quite a show of what he had in hand. "Then, all of a sudden, there he was on his knees before me," Block told the therapist, "and it didn't take very long . . . not the first time."

"And you let him do it more than once?"

"I think he sucked me off ten times in those four days."

"So you enjoyed it?"

"I don't know that I enjoyed it. It was something to do, and he liked doing it, so I let him, although I wondered what he was getting out of it. After we left the mountains, I cut him off . . . and then went into the Academy."

"Where you took up a chaste life."

"Damn chaste."

"But did you have fond memories of your four days in the mountains?"

"Not that I remember. In fact, I haven't thought about it in ten years."

The young man was now standing close at Block's side, his slender, glistening, clean erection not more than two inches from the side of Block's face. In his dreams, Kim's head from time to time withdrew from Lyons' crotch. Her fingers, nails painted crimson, held the slick, male rod upright, and more than once he believed it was longer and thicker than in previous dreams—a mighty cock with a big-domed, ridged head, a deep slash at the top of it, a hefty central tube bulging down the length of it, a cock the color of copper, the arched shaft filling Kim's encircling hand. It had never occurred to Block that it made much difference whether a man had four or nine inches, but in his dreams the size of what Lyons' had was important, however, only once, while dreaming, was he aware of any desire to touch it himself, to get the weight of it and feel its rigidity.

Under an acacia, the blond young man stood with his pelvis immediately before Block, and his right hand swayed his snake-thin erection. The major had to admit he wished it was Lyons. It was then he decided without equivocation that he didn't need a head shrink to uncover the fact that he had been sexually attracted to this particular sergeant, and that's that, he told himself. And this bravest of comrades had died, before I knew what it was I felt, before I could let him know how I felt. If it was he standing here instead of this nice, sexy kid, I suppose there'd be little doubt about what I'd want to do. Now I wish I'd done it before he was killed, before his mutilated body was lowered into a grave for insects to devour to the bones. Damn, Lyons, why didn't I? Would you have let me? Were you wanting me to when you stood in that lagoon in a bright shaft of light and let me see how much of a man you were?

The head of the youth's hardon was aimed at Block's mouth, almost touching it. Everyone looked to see if the visitor would accept it. He might have if the youth had anyway resembled Lyons. But he didn't. He's just a clean, long-haired kid, Block mused, a surfer type, maybe strung out on marijuana. I've seen that look in blue eyes before. In any case, he has no heft and toughness, no seasoned, manly substance. Does it make any difference now that I turned queer for Lyons? He is dead, and my cock is dead. Maybe dead for good. That piece of shrapnel I took maybe shattered some essential nerve. Tough luck!

He felt only curiosity when he watched the therapist and young woman leisurely couple on the grass. He watched the young fellow jack off, wished he could do the same and envied the load shot. But, a half hour later, when he drove away from the estate, he didn't dwell on the matter, nor on his impotency. Tough luck, he repeated in thought. Best not to be morbid about it. Presently he would have another mission to prepare for.

≠

It wasn't until he met a marine sergeant in a Manhattan hotel that his sexuality was fully revived. Before leaving for the Near East, Block was on short leave. He visited his son and daughter in Connecticut, saw Kim, too, without warming up to her, although he had hoped he would. She was friendly enough and eager for him to enjoy his children. However, he found, as often before, he didn't have much to say to a small boy, now five-years-old, and even less to a coy girl of three. So the visit was cut short, goodbyes were said and foreheads kissed. The soldier hoped that his ex-wife's second husband would do better by the kids in the ordinary, fatherly way and by the time he reached Manhattan, with the better part of a week to spend before returning to the base, Block had as good as forgotten his offspring and valued his detachment. For an hour or so he thought of catching a plane for London, where he had a lady friend, who would welcome him—but then, she'll want to fuck, and I can't, he said to himself and remained adrift in the tumult of the city.

As a lad, he'd often been in the swanker sections, for his mother had been an art dealer who had taken him to galleries, museums and concerts. So he did all that again, enjoying the Museum of Modern Art, again seeing the Cezanne's, Rousseau's and Matisse's—particularly the Rousseau's, which reminded him of his dreams of Kim blowing Lyons. He fell asleep during much of the third act of a Met *Die Gotterdammerung* but awoke in time for Brunnhilde's self-immolation and, an hour later, met a hooker in a cocktail lounge. A diminutive Asian in a sleek gown, she turned on at the sight of him in uniform, and he sat more than an hour listening to her fanciful chatter in superb English. He abstractly imagined himself making love to her, fondling cream-colored breasts, stroking the proverbial velvety thighs, but these erotic fancies left him unmoved. Nothing came of the encounter. Next evening, in civilian clothes, he wandered the seething streets on foot around Broadway and Times Square, curiously elated by the junky racket of taxis and derelict throng, the city noisier than battle—our democracy a wild, circus warfare, he mused, wondering if it were for this licentious, tawdry breed that he and men like Lyons fought. It doesn't matter. We do what we do. The rest do what they do. Seeing a marquee aglow advertising *Deep Throat,* he went inside and quickly saw what was being glorified on the silver screen; John Holmes' big one, five feet high, shimmering—so, Block mused, after two hundred centuries of Christianity burning and hacking its way to the top of the heap, paganism is still alive and well. Thousands throng to watch a blowjob. Toward dawn, walking to his hotel, he imagined that Sergeant Lyons walked at his side. The disciplined officer suddenly felt like a little boy with an imaginary friend—and what was Lyons saying? "Cocksucker. This is one of those nights I'd sure like to have my cock sucked."

The following afternoon, in an elevator, he met the gap-toothed, slightly homely, crew-cut, six-foot-two-inch or so hunk of a marine, and they wasted little time. The leatherneck, hand in his pocket, made an adjustment at his crotch. Block felt a distinctive stirring of his loins. By the time they had passed the ninth floor, it was clear neither of them would back away from their mutual attraction. It was lust at first sight. When the elevator got to the fourteenth floor, it stopped, and the door slid open. The jarhead's erection was delineated in his trousers, and he was grinning. "This is where I get out," Block said, "and it seems we have some unfinished business." In the deserted hallway, the marine's fly was hurriedly undone. Once they were in a room and its door had been shut, they yanked down each other's trousers, tossed shoes, socks, shirts and shorts and then crashed naked on a squeaking bed. Block held up the leatherneck's hardon; brownish-red, compacted, vein-gnarled, dense under its thin skin, the scrotum beneath large with testicles, the mat of hair framing it dark brown and kinky. With his face right to it and the smell of it full in his nostrils, Block felt it was the most significant thing he had ever beheld and couldn't remember when he had been so elated. It was larger than the room, larger than life.

A husky voice said, "Hey, man ... are you just going to look at it ... or start sucking." The marine quickly positioned himself to demonstrate how it was done, drawing Block's cock into his big, wet mouth, sucking it vigorously, getting it rigid. Within minutes, the novice, impotency broken, was ejaculating, the orgasm painful, as if some vital organ within had split, as if gut were being ripped out with the semen. But Block was unconcerned for he was intent on what he was doing, getting the hang of cocksucking, finding the right angle so that shaft and mouth were aligned properly, getting further down on it without gagging, accepting the back and forth pumping in his head, relishing the smell and taste of crotch, the memory of Lyons spurring him on. "That-a-way, man ... take it ... take it." When cum gushed into his throat, Block swallowed hard at it—and, in a desert, six years later, it was Corporal Riley who, his member submerged in the colonel's mouth, hissed through his clenched teeth, "Sir, I'm coming ... coming ... Jeeesuuuus." Not long after, the two sweating soldiers reclined in repose, seated on the narrow bunk, their backs to a wall as they listened to erratic wind outside and the dry flapping of agitated window shades.

"No doubt you'd like another drink. I need one to wash down your sperm."

Their mating was far from over, for, after they had napped off the hard edge of fatigue, they groggily awoke to one another. Block's hand strayed on the flesh and hair of the formidable leg beside him, which pressed closer, his mate letting him know he was awake to touch and willing to bestow himself again. The air had cooled, and there was intense darkness. The wind had died, so there was a permeating silence. Unseen, both cocks were up. Block cupped Riley's scrotum, and the corporal laid a heavy arm along the officer's shoulders in camaraderie. When the middle finger of Block's right hand found and massaged the fellow's warm anus, the corporal's legs parted further, and he shifted his weight to the small of his back so that he could lift his heavy butt, curve it somewhat upward to allow freer access to the tight orifice. Block knelt on the floor again and put his face to the rump. Riley knows what I want, he thought. He's taken the perfect position—maybe by instinct—maybe because that sergeant taught him in that warehouse. The colonel proceeded to inhale the earthy perfume. His tongue parted the hair around the sphincter and lapped on it—a tasty Eucharist, he thought. Riley sighed with contentment, and his hands pulled the two orbs further apart for Block's mouth to kiss, lick and suck into the moist seam.

"Jesus, sir ... does that ever feel nice. This is the first time anyone's ever done that."

"Not even the sergeant who admired you?"

"Well, he tried, but I wouldn't let him go that far."

The marine in the hotel had said, "Getting sucked is one thing ... sucking is another ... but when you get to smooching on a man's asshole, you know you've arrived. You've gotten to the heart of the matter."

Presently Riley's anus was relaxed and dilating, so the tip of Block's tongue darted into the fissure onto slick, inner tissue. He also sucked deeply at the hole with all his heart and mind, not letting up for long, long minutes. Riley's hands came to the back of the colonel's head, and he pushed onto it, holding the face to its feast. "God, I love that." After a while, he said. "You want to fuck me, don't you, sir?"

There was no need to answer.

Suddenly Riley had ahold of Block's erection and began pumping on it. "Shit, I'm hot, sir. I don't think I'd mind getting fucked by you ... would even like to get fucked by Colonel Block." His fist was slapping hard against his mate's pelvis. "I'd like you to shoot off in my ass, sir. But this bunk's kind of shaky. Let's do it on the floor where you can really throw it to me."

Three evenings later, in the same room, lights on, it was

blond, stacked Sergeant Kinsbursky who asserted himself into the corporal's rectum, sweat dripping from his brow, his biceps tense under smooth skin, his hands firmly holding the thighs before him, his face drained in spite of its tan, his motions dogged.

That afternoon, Kinsbursky—descended from Ukrainians—had let his commanding officer know he was used to and expected to be admired. The volunteers, led by Block, had traversed rocky terrain in glaring sunlight and had ascended a steep incline to a high plateau to a lookout above, if not Godless then a God-tormented wasteland. There they had rested. The men had broken rations open, eaten like wolves, guzzled water and stretched out on parched, shadeless ground. Dazed, no one had spoken for some time, then had grumbled sporadic obscenities, their voices comingled with sporadic gusts of wind from nowhere in the desolation under a cloudless, blanched sky, the men's talk aimless as the wind. They were at a turning point, with fifteen miles to recross before they arrived at their barracks again. Before telling his unit to get to its feet, Block moved to the cliff's edge, dizzily looked down at boulders three hundred feet below, scanned the panoramic, hostile horizon and opened his fly to urinate, aiming the glinting stream over the side. His wits abuzz, he was slow to perceive that someone had come forward and was standing near him in the relentless light, slow to recognize Sergeant Kinsbursky, who was also pissing. The fellow gyrated the stream in loops, and this boyish gesture amused the colonel. He smiled broadly—perhaps a little crazily, he thought. Kinsbursky then made quite a show of milking off the last drops of liquid, then standing there with a semi-erection. An abrupt gust of wind swirled around the two men, and the blond said, "It sure feels good getting it out ... letting it all hang out."

"Yes," the colonel answered. To himself, he thought, in spite of hardships, awful war and a desolate man-scorching desert, we are eternally horny. And, by the look of Kinsbursky, he knows precisely what can and should be done between two men.

Late that night, after their return to the forlorn base, Block called the corporal and sergeant to his quarters, where the savvy son of Slavs, beyond the call of duty after an arduous day, was quick to strip. When both young men were naked, the colonel thought they looked like knights awaiting investiture. To limber their aching bodies, he massaged necks, backs, and the length of arms, the rounds of rumps too. Drenching a towel several times with tepid water from a faucet, the officer, the military priest, freely applied the liquid to their bodies and washed away sweat and grime. Soon flesh was glistening. All cocks were up. It was then Riley laid on the desktop, drew his bent knees toward his chest and offered his bowed buttocks, agreeable to being primed with lubricant. When the burnished hole was completely greased, Block gestured Kinsbursky forward to give his best. In silence, the sergeant looked down to where a sphincter was wrapped around the creamy extension of himself, the muscle caving in with each penetration, the lips clinging to the shaft each time it drew back. Twice the cock slipped out and sprang up, flinging off a drop of fluid. But Kinsbursky was quick to reinsert the hard mass. Block lowered his head and placed the tip of his tongue to where anal and genital tissue coupled—tasting of man and man in communion, he meditated—one man giving, the other taking, without equivocation.

Just as Kinsbursky began to climax, he implored, "You want me to shoot off in his butt . . . or give it to you in the mouth, sir?" Pulled from the hole, his already discharging cock was hastily directed toward Block's lips, open in an O. After the sergeant's wrenching had subsided, the colonel turned to lap up traces of semen which clung to Riley's anus—his holy butt-hole, and this I do in honor of Lyons, who had a stake rammed up his. Then Kinsbursky, still feisty, got up on the desk and took the same position the corporal had, saying, "It's been a long, long time since I've had a rimming. Love to be rimmed." So Block had two anuses to relish, one dark and hairy, the other almost hairless and the color of a sunburnt peach—two altars to kneel before, he observed silently—and Christ, Lyons, I wish I had kissed your asshole before you died. Presently it was clear, Kinsbursky wanted more than a rimming, for he reached down, placed one of Block's finger in the right spot and forced it into his rectum. More lubricant was applied. The finger was soon submerged to the hilt, revolving, rectal tissue coaxed. Riley, after gazing at the Slav's crotch with bewilderment, lowered his head and drew on the organ, which only minutes before had been buried in his own ass, and presently he was sucking on it zealously. Block said to himself, once the hunger of man for man is unleashed in the psyche, it is formidable.

Moments later he spoke aloud to Riley, "Okay, my chap . . . it's your turn. Let's see if Kinsbursky is as good a sport as you." The rangy, silent, auburn-haired man to got his feet, took his position at the butt and slipped in his erection. He humped with increased momentum, soon the flesh of his pelvis slapping against the flesh of the sergeant's rump, his big frame jarring his prone comrade. A hefty fuck, Block observed, getting atop the desk alongside the blond and taking the same position, so Riley could alternate between the two of them. Glorying in the sensation of a hard, slick cock thrusting into him and while staring at the ceiling, he began to perceive of how he would arrange all twenty of his volunteers so that each would join with each. That night the idea was only half formed. Over the next few days, it would all fall into place, exactly how his men would muster to share in a ribald, ballsy, Spartan requiem for fallen soldiers—and the living too. He wouldn't rest until he hit upon the exact formation they should take. He would be driven until it was achieved. It would be the last, great act of his life, or so he believed.

TWO

Reveille blasted over a loudspeaker, the taped bugle call cracking the desert's crystal silence. After this jolt, Master-Sergeant Marshall, Block's aid, barked, "Out of your sacks. Drop your dongs and hit the floor. As far as we know, the fucking enemy is over the hill, and this is our last day on earth. On the double. No time to gripe. No time to piss, shit or dress. On the double . . . out onto the compound."

After hearing a confusion of heavy feet on floorboards, the colonel listened to muster from his room. "Bain." "Yo." "Bartolatta." "Yeah." "Campbell." From the open window, he couldn't make out the details of the men as the grounds were without illumination except for an indistinct glimmering of sun at the eastern horizon. But the look of the bunch was etched in his mind, for he'd seen hundreds of such clusters and hand picked this unit. "Dimick." "Yo." "Dunning." "Here." The replies became heartier after the rude awakening was shaken off. Block was moved by the fact that some men still responded to this call to stand at attention in dawn's light and be counted. His heart stirred even more lately since there was reason to wonder why anyone would bother to rally, since neither side was winning the war and the complex machinations ordered by remote chiefs of staff had proven to be hardly more than complicated failures. Many men had said to hell with it and left, to find what was left of families among a disorganized civilian population. "Ferguson." "Yo." "Flannery." "Yah." "Gerald." The previous morning they had run the obstacle course nude, the colonel having said to them simply, "We drop our shorts to screw . . . so why not do the same as we break our butts one more time." They had come from their bunks on the rush clad only in skivvies. He'd stripped before them, then took off at a run, not looking back to see if anyone followed: he knew they would. Morning air cool on his armpits, Block went hand over hand up a rope, lifting the weight of his body straight up sixty feet, then swung onto a taut line stretched at an angle to the ground. Halfway down, he dropped, to sprint again, to glance back and see the pack of joggers under an expanding, pearly light.

At twenty, Tom Block had won a medal at the '84 Olympic Games, pitting his body against the record. His frequent reading of history informed him that in the first Olympiad, eight centuries before Christ, the footrace had been a mere two hundred yards: in later years the distance was increased to half a mile, and, later, the contestants ran the circumference of the stadium twelve times—two-and-a-half miles. The Spartans set the fashion of doing it naked, proudly. In this first year of the twenty-first century, none of his twenty volunteers, twenty-two counting Marshal and himself, had balked at taking the course bareassed, though some may have resented the command. However not a one had anything to be ashamed of, and he had chosen each, not only for his intelligence and accomplishments in the field, but also for stamina, physique and genital size. He'd been present during the medical examinations of over a hundred volunteers and had made his selection on the basis of those five criteria. They were a bunch of rugged, brainy cocksmen.

Running, he heard pounding feet catching up to him, and with a sideways look, caught sight of Romero's profile coming into view. Romero, the Chicano, more Indian than Spanish, was about to overtake him as they ran toward the next obstacle—rows of thigh-high hurdles to be taken at a dash. Rather than pull ahead, Romero began to slacken, perhaps in respect for the colonel's status, but Block's voice jabbed the air, "If you can outrun me . . . do it!" After they took ten hurdles, Romero, dark-skinned and fleet of legs, surged forward, getting more than a yard on the officer in a burst. However he could not maintain the lead for long, since Block got a second wind—as in a Manhattan hotel six years before, he'd gotten a deep, second wind, a new hold on life given to him by a marine, the two lingering in a bed licking a residue of saliva and semen off each other's genitals. The initiate hadn't felt any less a man for having done what he'd just done, instead felt a renewed sense of manliness, whatever that was, while he had closely scrutinized every detail of the crotch immediately before his face: the rubbery texture of the ridged cockhead, its deeply cut, pink mouth, the network of loose veins on the rotund shaft under its thin, brownish, outer membrane; had inspected every wrinkle of the scrotum and the sprouts of hair on it; had contemplated the round, dark anus below the testicles and studied the striations of the sphincter, the strongest muscle of the human body. He had worked up another erection on the man, held it by the thick base and slapped it back and forth across his cheeks and nose, while inhaling a musky aroma. This is raw male, and I love it.

The jarhead, laughing, had said, "I suppose you're wondering what we do for repeats."

"It's crossed my mind."

"Ever been to The Stud's Pen?"

"What is that?"

"A bar . . . a club. A pit, where you can have all the repeats you need . . . suck and fuck all night. Want to come with me?"

"Why not."

"I can tell you're pretty new at this, so maybe you need your baptism in cum."

Years later, dawn was enlarging behind a distant, silhouetted mountain range with effusive blue, the jagged masses of earth primeval, formidable, inhuman, while the sight of Romero's compact, limber, gleaming body beside him was congenial. The two of them, still ahead of the others, pranced through a maze of discarded auto tires, their pebble-bruised feet landing in the center of the black circles, peckers flopping. Comrades were immediately behind, sweat trickling, abdomen's flat, pain a spur. You have to keep your breathing steady, lungs coordinated with legs, or you'll break down in confusion, Block had reminded himself many times. At West Point, he'd been called a gazelle, "the lonely, long distance fool;" and he called the last quarter-mile the heartbreak, ass-breaking sprint—but when you win there's a crazy euphoria, your heart pounding like a hunger-driven cheetah's.

The last volunteer came to a halt in a muddle of men, and Block began doing knee-bends, squatting, rising, squatting, rising. After forty, he positioned himself for pushups, back rigid, arms taut. Up and down, up and down; the touch of air in the crack of his buttocks was invigorating; up and down, forty times, then five more—I push myself to the limit, therefore I exist. At the periphery of his vision, the mountain range rose and fell, and Block was delighted by glimpses of the muscle flexing butts nearest him, the thick rumps of big men, the central seams deep and dark—and, in a hotel, he had studied the marine sergeant's broad rump. The leatherneck had said, "Before we go to *The Studs' Pen,* I'm going up to my room and take a douche, a huge enema."

Tom Block had laughed. "Why in hell?"

"Because I mean to get fucked tonight . . . plenty . . . and I want it clean."

Upstairs, the big fellow had bent over, and in the novice's eyes, the dense butt he beheld, had seemed to become larger than the small bathroom. On one cheek there'd been tattooed a swastika, its arms reverse to the Nazi's, like the swastika seen on Indian teepees. Both the muscular mounds had been tanned, indicating the sergeant had been sunbathing nude. The leatherneck had reached back and pulled them apart, the center fold hair-filled, and Block had been given the honor of separating the hair around the blackish-brown anus and of inserting the greased, plastic nozzle. After the man's belly had bloated and he'd sat on a toilet, the officer, thinking his companion would want privacy in which to relieve himself, left the room. However, over the sound of a flush, a voice had called him back. "Does the smell of shit make you squeamish or something? Come in. Let me have another look at you. What you lack in size, you make up in muscle. Lean and mean, man. Turn around. Bend over. Ever have your asshole eaten out?"

"No."

"Well, you're about to now. But first, why don't you have a douche? We'll get it good and clean."

"Why not."

"Goldstein." "Yo." "Holmes." The husky Jew and the tall, supple Black were the last two in the front line, Kinsbursky the first in the next, not in the least embarrassed by nudity—a happy exhibitionist, the colonel thought and then asked aloud, "Sergeant, why did you volunteer?"

"To serve Colonel Block. If I may ask ... why are you leading us?"

"It is my karma ... or else I'm stark, raving stupid."

There was no reply to that.

"That Scotsman beside you is a rough-looking customer."

"Right out of the wild boonies, sir."

"McCormick." "Yo." This gangly guy was not only hairy in the usual places but had irregular, reddish swatches on his neck, shoulders and thighs.

"Do you feel foolish standing out here bareassed?"

"Not particularly, sir."

At the end of his dangling cock, the glans penis was half emerged from the foreskin.

"Do you know the Spartans of old thought nothing of going into battle naked?"

"Spartans?"

"Greeks from the city of Sparta who warred with Athens for nearly thirty years."

A trace of a smile came to McCormick's lank face. "Those Greeks were cornholers, weren't they, sir?"

"I've heard it said."

Block's male organ was one quarter up. While he and McCormick shared an understanding through their eyes, in the morning's growing luminosity, the remainder of the tall fellow's cockhead slipped from its foreskin. He won't hesitate when the time comes, the officer thought; he'll jump into the fray. Was it time to initiate it? No.

"Rappaport." "Here." He was the handsomest of the bunch, in a sultry, French way—doubtless a lady-killer. He was not gregarious, and Block wondered if he would disdain the bonding rites intended for these men. After all, most men had been conditioned to feel that their sexuality was a private matter, something to be expressed behind closed doors with a single partner and not openly aired. The colonel could not hope that all would willingly enter into his plan—however they are good soldiers, and the best invariably pick up the gauntlet when it is tossed before them.

When they were recruits, the Army had shorn their hair, made skinheads of them, taken away their hodgepodge of civilian garb, tossed identical government issue at them, had slapped identical chow for them to eat off identical metal trays, then drilled them in unison: hundreds expected to present arms as one on command, to sleep under identical, woolen blankets on sparse mattresses on mass-produced steel racks. They showered and shaved together, shit and pissed side by side, no privacy except in dreams. Squads of them were forged in undeviating sameness, paced through routines and regulations to make cohesive, disciplined units of men who had been motley, irregular civilians. The miracle, in Block's view, was that none of them became robots. Individualism is too deeply ingrained in the men of our country to be given up, he thought: an individualism which the Army didn't care to eradicate in the belief that such men made more effective fighters. So that muster—apart from being a counting of heads—gave each a chance to individually respond to the calling out of his name: "Campbell," "Dimick," "Dunning," and now "Rappaport." Each let it be known that he was present, able, ready and very much himself.

Also, in spite of the fact that all had essentially the same anatomy, there was a variety of physical differences. Two were golden-haired, Gerald with a crowning mass of ringlets. Others had straight hair, brown and black, and several men were balding. Then, too, there were differing skin textures; several appeared leathery, and the youngest still had resilient flesh. Then, varying amounts of body hair; some grossly hirsute, and those with hair so perfectly arranged on chests, forearms and legs it seemed the work of an artist, while smooth-skinned Kinsbursky and Gerald looked almost as naked as skinned rabbits. Some men were burly, others rangy, and there were those who had classic proportions. There were a variety of noses: perfectly straight, pug, hooked and broken. Some had high cheekbones; some oval faces as opposed to those who had square faces. Each was made unique by the cut of its mouth, the shape of lips, the set of jaws, the width and angle of forehead and the size of its ears on either side. There were the plain, handsome, homely and baby-faced. And if more difference was wanted, a look into twenty pairs of eyes showed each man's history and spirit; smiling eyes, passive eyes, stern eyes, inquisitive eyes, here and there a gleam of cruelty in a pair.

"Riley." "Yo." On his face was a fleeting expression of love, or excruciating tenderness.

"Romero." "Yo." He was the shortest of the men yet with arms as powerful as any, his barrel-chest the most striking feature.

"Well, you outdistanced me twice."

The man's brown face remained intently serious.

"The Incas used to have runners who carried messages for their rulers high in the Andes, running pell-mell from village to village on mountain passes. Incredible endurance up there in that thin air," Block said. "They were veritable running machines."

"That is why many of us Indios have big chests, sir."

"Do you run in honor of your people?"

"I run for myself."

And will he throw himself into our spartan orgy? Block asked himself. Of the ten sets of genitals in this row of men,

Romero's was the fattest and darkest, and he seemed unconcerned about displaying it. There's no timidity in him.

"Saunders." This man, once tried but acquitted on a charge of murder, had a look of an unconscionable brute; no enlivening curiosity in his eyes, instead a stoniness—and I wonder what it is he holds so tenaciously to himself. He has proven himself many times but scoffs at honors. It was a woman he allegedly killed. Maybe he did. There's ferocity in him, but no hate. I think he will be the hardest to win over.

Next to him was Tullius, a musclebuilder, a lug of an Italian with glinting black hair and a pockmarked, although not unhandsome, face. The previous day, he and Block had encountered each other during a break in the march. Tullius had his pants down and was squatting, having just dropped a hard turd from his suspended buttocks. Seeing that he'd caught Block's eye, he had taken his time wiping himself with gingerly applied dust from a clod he'd crumbled, then he'd stood and stepped forward out of the shade which diagonally cut across a brushy ravine, into light; the chalky white light of a Manet painting, Block had observed. Rather than cover up immediately, Tullius had let his trousers remain at his knees, the muscles of his forelegs bulging, his cock's dome the color of oxblood shoe polish—a macho Narcissus, if I read him correctly, Block had thought. Taking the scene further, the Italian had cupped his scrotum and given it a lift. Three nearby soldiers had watched, perhaps speculating on the next move, and the colonel had been tempted to walk to Tullius, get the taunting cock in hand and thereby let the onlookers know, in broad daylight, that he was driven by more than preparing them to meet the enemy. It would be simple enough—I need only kneel before that crotch. However, a smirk had turned the corners of Tullius' thick, brownish lips. Block had stopped short, turned away and left the man to wonder if his impertinence had been misgauged.

But the Italian wasn't rebuffed. Next morning at muster, he was no less cocksure, awaiting the review of his commanding officer with his male member at half-mast, more than seven inches on the verge of a complete erection. A fireball sun hung over the eastern mountains, their twisted convolutions in high relief. Pink-orange-red flushed the undersides of flat clouds, and the shadows of men's torsos, legs, heads and arms were long and tangled on the flat compound. Block stood directly before Tullius and moved closer, so that his abdomen touched the blunt end of the soldier's cock, so the organ had to move either downward or upward. It did the latter, and the two stood with their erections side by side. The colonel's eyes remained unswerving and cold when he spoke; "I suppose your ancestors marched in Imperial Rome's phalanxes. Have you ever wondered why those men spent most of their short lives at war?"

"I've heard it was for the loot."

Tullius had not properly addressed his superior so was reprimanded. "The form of address is ... Sir."

" ... for the loot, sir."

"But in the wreckage of our wars, there is no bounty, and pay is slow in coming."

"They've taken the glory out of it."

"One general once said that war is hell ... and another said it is heaven. Which do you think it is?"

"I don't know."

"It is probably no more than a matter of fact."

They were standing so close the hair of their crotches brushed. Block's tone had made it seem he was dressing the man down, however he admired him, smiled and said, "Well, whatever war is, I see you're not without pride. Is that a piss hardon you've got, or do you usually greet the sun amorously?"

"Amorously?"

"With love?"

"If you mean, would I like to throw a hard fuck right now ... the answer is yes."

"Sir."

"Sir."

Two men down the line laughed but cut it short. Tullius stood tall, biceps bunched, pectorals in high relief in the slanted sunlight, the man bristling with vanity, and Block knew it would be simple for him to turn, offer his backsides and thus make clear what he meant the volunteers to know collectively—but at the right time, in the right way. He was no Caligula, who had Praetorean guards sodomize him before members of his court to satisfy some insane whim. What he wanted was a fulfillment of heartfelt comradeship, a fraternity of virile warriors. In any case, he'd already decided the way in which he would reveal his purpose, in the light of day, under a blue sky, before all. In the meantime, he withdrew from Tullius, went to the last man and considered the much-battered face of ex-pugilist Vild.

≠

After a glance from his commander, Master-sergeant Marshall called the soldiers to break ranks and pair off for wrestling. In ancient Greece, at the twelfth or some other Olympiad, discus and javelin throwing had been added to the events. More than a decade later, fist-fighting and wrestling, too, as the Games became more warlike. If not before, from then on, there had been three-thousand years of male competition, some tame as a tennis match, some awful as World War I when half the young men of Europe had been maimed, deranged or killed. In this patriarchal epoch, men were instinctively combative—whether in a collosseum, a stock exchange, or war between city states. Perhaps it had become part of the genetic makeup of men, Western men anyway—and there's not much point in arguing it, Block believed. Also, what made a crack fighting unit, such as the several he had created in his fifteen years of leadership, was that this inherent competitiveness could be improved with male bonding, the bonding of rigorous individualists, who left to their own devices would fight one another, but when brought together forged an impressive company. and the ritual of comrades wrestling amongst themselves was a quintessential, artistic expression of this duality—and I hope to strip all vestiges of hypocrisy and subterfuge. I have asked them to do this in the nude.

The colonel singled out Dimick for his opponent, largest and swarthiest of the pack, four inches taller than Block, more than twenty pounds heavier, his head half bald, shaped like a blunt missile, his face, with an untamed mustache, suggesting some fierce Tartar warrior, and his skin glistening as though it had taken a hard polish. He was also chosen because of his abnormally thick cock, it being the biggest of the twenty-two in the unit, even in its present limp state hanging about four inches long, more than two across, its circumsized head appearing weighty. However, in spite of his impressive bulk, Dimick seemed to have some hesitation about taking on Block, who quickly said, "Forget about my rank. At this we are equals. I expect you to give it your all." On flexed, slightly bent legs, the colonel weaved before the powerhouse, ready to dodge should his opponent make the initial lunge, and, in this feigning position, he twice swiped at his own cock, which was erect, and it seemed he was luring Dimick to a sexual contest instead of a wrestling match. But then, unexpectedly, he sprang with the agility of a lioness, got behind the man, twisted an arm into a locked position and strained to topple the formidable form. Dimick then hurtled him off, up and over his bent shoulders and head. Block landed on his feet and quickly sidestepped when the body charged him. Meeting only thin air, Dimick lost his balance and fell. Block abruptly dropped onto his midsection, however this was swiftly reversed, and Dimick's bare butt was hard on the colonel's chest, his weight moved forward to pin the shoulders down, his crotch posed at the prone throat. Apparently thinking he had already won the match, Dimick looked triumphantly into the eyes below him, however the officer smiled and brought his mouth to the bulging scrotum near it. This took the sitting man off guard, and a worried expression crossed his whisker-stubbled, rough-cut, slant-eyed face with the idea that his wily foe might fight dirty, might even bite his balls. To protect them, he arose slightly, and this gave Block the advantage he sought. The colonel lifted his legs high and got them around Dimick's throat, interlocked them and pulled his adversary backward. After vigorous seesawing, they found themselves on their sides, each with his legs around the other's neck, each with his face at a butt. With prying hands, Block parted the broad, dense mounds, and then blew a gust of air to part the tangled hair around a rather large, gnarled, leathery-looking anus. He applied a lapping tongue to it, and Dimick went stiff, momentarily shocked throughout, but Block persisted licking and giving the fissure friendly gooses with the tip of his nose, disarming his opponent, who released the pressure on the colonel's neck. Freed, Block raised his head over the crotch, got a handful of cock, began stroking motions, watched it elongate and felt it harden against his palm. It promised to be as great as the one displayed in Manhattan once, at a place called *The Studs' Pen,* at a cock measuring contest, when the winner had come in with one nine inches long, three inches across its flat upper side, and, more important, nine inches all around. Diligently as several admirers had tried, few had been able to get their mouths further than halfway on the shaft. Major Block had done best at this and, now, in a desert, on the ground, in the broad light of day, in view of anyone who cared to look, was preparing to go down on Dimick's hardon. This was how he'd decided to announce to all his volunteers that Colonel Thomas Block—athlete, long-distance runner, winner of an Olympic gold medal—leader of men, lion of the Army, honored for bravery with oak leaf clusters—daredevil of many deadly missions—was, among other things, a cock-sucker, not in the least reluctant to celebrate with gusto a horny brother-in-arms.

His lips encircled the cockhead, and the taste of it soon dispelled the dryness of his mouth with a flow of saliva so that he was able to glide down on more. Dimick began to relax. The legs around his neck loosened their grip, and his head lay upon the soil, his eyes rolling to the blue sky above. He raised his pelvis toward the sucking mouth, and his hands went to the back of the head lowered to him, holding it in place. After having gotten two-thirds down the elongated mass, Block disengaged himself in order to hold it up and lick it from the hair surrounding its base to its top, and this he did so that anyone, who cared to look, would knew he relished the primeval essence of male.

However, least anyone forget his reputation, he suddenly jumped to his feet and baited Dimick to do the same so they could resume the match. The big man was slow to get to his feet. The two of them face to face again, Block weaved from side to side. Dimick came from his temporary daze, and both sized each other up again, seeking an advantage. Twice the officer shook his erection; twice Dimick imitated him; and the match was resumed. The bigger of the two lifted the smaller off his feet in a bear-hug, which might have become affectionate if Block's hands hadn't criss-crossed his adversary's throat at the windpipe, causing Dimick's head to tilt backward until he lost his balance and toppled, bringing the officer down with him. They hit the ground with a thud, Block squirming to fix his lean rump atop the hair-matted chest then placing his ass to throat, his erect cock at Dimick's line of sight.

≠

When Marshall called a halt to the exercise, the match could be judged a draw. The other wrestlers stood panting and squirming, and the master-sergeant shouted, "You've got twenty minutes before we begin today's march. No time to shower or shave. No time for chow. We're going empty belly. Just time enough to piss and crap . . . have a cigarette and dress. The uniform of the day is on your bunks. Get going. You mothers have got twenty minutes.

Moments later, in the crowded john, Dimick stood at a urinal pointing his erection down, pissing a strong stream, feeling like a man who had just been knighted by a king, under his breath saying, "Christ, I'm glad Block did that." It certainly wasn't the first time his cock had been sought. At twenty, down and out, he'd answered an ad in a porn magazine, "And the next thing I knew I was getting photographed in the raw," he'd told a confidante in drunkenness one night. "And next think I knew I was in a fuck flick ... laying back letting broads suck on it ... or try to ... most of them not able to get much more than the head in. And I got paid for it. Then the fags got hold of me. Shit, my whanger was up in centerfolds all over the country. I went solo in one half-hour flick, jacking off and coming, jacking off and coming ... and they told me people were watching my cum shots all over the world. Back then I could pick up a hundred bucks just to let people play with it. One old gal told me she oughta put a bonnet on it and hug it. More than once I was the star attraction at parties ... paid to come out naked and beat my meat. Shit, I had it down to a science. I could flog it for a long, long time and hold off coming until most of the guests were half crazy wanting to see me shoot off. Then I'd lay back and let everyone come suck my nuts and lick on the old whanger."

However Dimick had abruptly dropped out of all this, not understanding why. "Maybe because I was ashamed of whoring ... because that's what I was doing ... and drinking too much. All of a sudden I got married, got a job as a plumber and straightened myself out ... for a while. But, shit, my sex life with the little woman turned out to be a nightmare. The size of my whanger scared her. She couldn't take it all. If I got much more than the head in, she'd start whining. Why she hitched with me in the first place I'll never know. The next thing I knew she was cheating on me, so I left her. I fell in with the fags again ... doing it for money ... and drinking too much. I'll say one thing for the queers ... they suck a lot better than women do. One fag photographer told me, 'Sweetie, you have to have one to really hunger for one.' Well, anyway, it was a good thing the Army called me up and gave me something to do ... because I was becoming a mess fast."

Eight years later, in the desert, in a barracks john, he milked off the last of the urine and turned from the urinal and displayed his erection for any who cared to have a good look at it.

Dunning observed, "That cock of yours is an unnatural growth ... a tumor."

"You man enough to take it up the bunger?"

"Your mother must have fed you something special for you to grow something like that."

"She fed me elepant whang ... every morning on a dirty tray."

A rare liveliness crackled among the men in the john that morning. Perhaps the nude wrestling had turned them on, or what all had seen Block do with Dimick. In any case, their customary griping was more humorous than usual. Saunders, sitting on a toilet, turned to Ferguson beside him and asked, "Is that you who smells like a sewer?"

"I cannot tell a lie. But I know you don't shit roses."

Bain, enthroned three stools down, said, "By the numbers ... one, two, three ... shit." He grunted and grimaced.

Rappaport appraised his face in a mirror and rubbed his dark stubble with one hand as his other turned the hot water faucet. When it only sputtered, he grumbled, "What the hell! No hot water! Did they shut the fucker off?"

Dunning responded. "You heard what Marshall said." He imitated the master-sergeant's bellow. "No time to shower or shave ... just time enough to piss and crap."

"What kind of fucked up outfit is this? Making us prance around bareassed like a bunch of fairy recruits."

"By the numbers ... one, two, three ... flush."

Ferguson stood considering the turd he'd just emitted. "Longer than a rakehandle."

"Look at Tullius. He's still got a bone on."

The Italian waved it. "Like it, babe?"

Curly, blond-haired Gerald snatched two furtive glances

at it and at Tullius' face, his cock coming up in response.

It was contagious. Presently eight men were sporting erections. The male members of others were at half mast, bobbing as they walked.

"No time to shave or shower. Is there time to jack off?"

In the bunkroom, there was more joking when the volunteers saw the clothes set out on their racks; pith helmets, heavy sandals and leggings, and, to their consternation, khaki-colored tunics of coarse cloth.

Bartollatta, holding up his, exclaimed. "What the fuck! Dresses!" He raised his arm and let the tunic fall into place, the short-sleeved garb's lower hem covering his crotch by no more than two inches.

"No underwear," a voice noted.

"Nothing like letting it hang loose."

Goldstein laughed at lanky McCormick in his new uniform. "The hairiest dame I ever saw. Kind of cute though."

"Don't bend over. Butt mooning from a dress turns me on quicker than hell."

Ferguson hiked a leg and let a long, groaning fart.

"You must have the vilest bowels in creation."

"I've won a few farting contests."

"Jesus Christ! What a raunchy crew."

Dimick shimmied into his outfit, and the hem came to rest at the base of his upright tool. Beside him, Kinsbursky donned his tunic, did some quick kneebends and, each time he arose, followed with pelvic grinds, lifting his skirt and flashing. Clowning, he got hold of his erection and boyishly jerked on it several times. Dimick wasn't to be outdone and began on his own with serious intent. Tullius joined them; then McCormick, who came forward grinning. To everyone's surprise, the usually sullen Saunders took up the beat too, the fifth in line.

Kinsbursky laughed and said, "Nothing like a mass jack."

Bain urged, "By the numbers ... one, two, three ... beat that meat."

"Any bets on who comes first and most."

"I'll put a buck on Dimick. Beat it, you animal."

Dimick was doing just that without respite, and the other four became determined.

"One, two, three ... pound that pud."

Scarlet cockheads gyrated above the agitated fists. Testicles lurched from side to side and slapped against the flesh of legs. Men in search of release.

"By the numbers ... flog that dog."

Grunting, McCormick shot off first, instantly followed by Dimick. The first three globs of his ejaculation flew about two feet, and he milked for more, getting eight surges of semen. Saunders was third, his first wad breaking apart on impact against an onlooker's leg. Kinsbursky broke off from his exercise long enough to climb up to the top of a two-tiered bunk, where he resumed his exhibition, asking, "Anyone want a shower?" His member was whipped from side to side while it spurted cum. Tullius took longer in a labor of love, drawing his hand slowly up from the base, pulling up foreskin, drawing it down, then revolving his palm on his glistening, almost purple glans penis. This was repeated several times, while the fingers of his other hand rubbed fondly into the mats of hair over his pectorals. Momentarily he laid off and displayed the length of his cock in full view, while he looked from side to side saying, "Anyone want to eat it? There's bound to be three or four cocksuckers among us." Seeing the expression on Gerald's face, he went on, "I know you've been wanting to suck this for days, and you know I know ... and everyone else has figured it out. So get over here, babe. It's yours."

"By the numbers ... e-jac-u-late."

There was a burst of laughter when Gerald spontaneously shot off without even having touched himself. Immediately thereafter, Tullius quickly finished himself off, pointing his rigid member upward so that the nine eruptions of viscous stuff leapt straight up, the first four as high as his sunburnt neck.

Suddenly Dunning began working on himself, and it took

him about a quarter of a minute to climax.

Master-sergeant Marshall, after watching this with keen admiration and then seeing that the heat of the moment had subsided, shouted, "Okay ... drop your dongs. Out on the compound. Your twenty minutes are up. No more play. Time to meet the colonel."

Outside, the wisecracks were cut short. In harsh light, all the men stood with straight faces for Block's review. He, dressed as they were, once again went down the two lines. They were to resume survival exercises, this time to test themselves in the desert four days and nights. They would carry scant supplies and live off the land. An automatic weapon and canteen were hung from each pair of shoulders, and, because all were in their husky prime, none looked absurd in the tunics. "It's what the Spartans wore when they took to the field," was all the officer said by way of explanation. Soon they marched away two abreast, into the heat which had already set in.

≠

Late that afternoon, the sky darkened with thunderheads, and the air grew densely humid. More sweat wet the men's hair inside their helmets, slicked their brows and the cheeks of their morose faces, trickled down their necks and slithered down hairy legs. Then there was lightning, awesome flashes of it, followed by the booming of thunder. The air became turbulent and momentarily there was a cloudburst, heavy rain relentlessly pouring down. Sergeant Kinsbursky was the first to break ranks, to toss off his hat and tunic, to raise his arms so his armpits were flushed out, to bend over so the seam of his rump was doused. Tullius was the next to get naked. After Block disrobed, the remainder did the same, and presently everyone was delighting in the cleansing rain, their former doggedness in the march replaced by a growing merriment, big feet stomping in rushing water. The colonel singled out Dimick again as if the meant to resume their wrestling match, their glistening, slippery arms soon interlocked. Here and there grab-assing began among the volunteers, at first tentative, then more roughly as erections began to spring up. Block reached for his fallen knapsack, felt around inside it and then produced a large jar of vaseline, which he handed to Dimick, saying, "Of course you know I expect you to fuck me ... here ... now." He turned, bent slightly and placed his palms on his knees, his butt presented to Dimick, who, water drenching his face, looked dumbfounded, staring at the jar in his hand. "Prime me, man. Prime me."

"You sure, sir?"

"Very sure."

"I'm awfully big. It's likely to hurt you, sir."

"Which will make it all the more meaningful. Get to it. I've taken some as big as yours."

And he had. In The Studs' Pen, which he had visited often between missions over the years, one night, after a cock measuring contest, there had been a second contest, to see who could take the winner's big one up the ass. Block, bent, his palms flat on his bent knees, had been able to take it all, the pain fierce, but he was conditioned to pain, on the athletic field, during endurance tests, on the long haul before, during and after battle. Since his initiation in a Manhattan hotel, he'd learned to love the feel of hard cock in him, the turgid slip and slide of it, the assertive thrusting of a fellow man. It's like having brotherhood slammed up your ass, he'd mused. There had been applause among spectators in *The Studs' Pen*. Maybe they'll give me a gold medal for this. The flash of a photographer's camera had focused on the union, and Block's partner, after climaxing, after his gasping had ceased, had said, "Jesus man ... Jesus ... that's about the best I ever had. Me and you ought to get married." In fact they had spent the better part of the week together, honeymooning, Block taking a jamming up the ass as often as his big bedfellow mustered up his resolve. "Fuck me. Lyons, fuck me."

"Who's this Lyons you keep talking about?"

"You are Lyons, so fuck me." Block had sat on the big cock, another time taking it from behind dog fashion, or had lain on his back with his legs wrapped around the waist of the torso arched over him, and on the last morning they had taken turns at one another for the better part of two hours, laying off from time to time. "We eat out each other's assholes, therefore we are. We fuck each other and rejoice in bewilderment."

In the cloudburst, the colonel pushed against Dimick's slow, massive insertion and he thought of Lyons being impaled on a stake. Then glancing about, he saw that others had sought out partners. Curly-haired Gerald was on his knees before Tullius giving him a blowjob. The vaseline had been passed on, and gangly McCormick was taking Vild anally, getting himself cornholed, Block observed with a smile. Marshall was sucking on Holmes' black cock. Rappaport and Dunning were vying with one another to determine who would acquiesce to the other's urgency first. There were zaps of more lightning and a drumming of thunder. Another cloud seemed to tear asunder, releasing its weight of water, and wind whipped in every direction. For several moments the naked, agitated men seemed to be afloat, then in some antic, lusty dance. Two fell to the ground and began avidly sixty-nining with one another. Saunders came forward and stood before Block, looking down at the erection he presented. "You want to suck it, colonel?" His voice was poignant, and the expression in his usually hard eyes was all tenderness, so presently Block had a cock in his mouth and one humping within his rectum. Those men, who didn't seek partners, stood here and there beating on their male meat, so this company of men were proving itself to be everything the colonel had hoped for, a band of virile, cock-proud men. The storm had torn away all inhibitions. The lightning had charged libidos. The thunder was spurring them to climaxes. Dimick became more forceful, his thrusts jarring Block. Then he was groaning, "I'm coming, sir. I'm coming. Take my load." Moments later Saunders, though usually intensely silent, was loquacious. "Love it . . . love it . . . love it. Nothing better than a good cock sucking. And here it comes. Take my beautiful stuff."

Spirits were buoyant in the gloomy light.

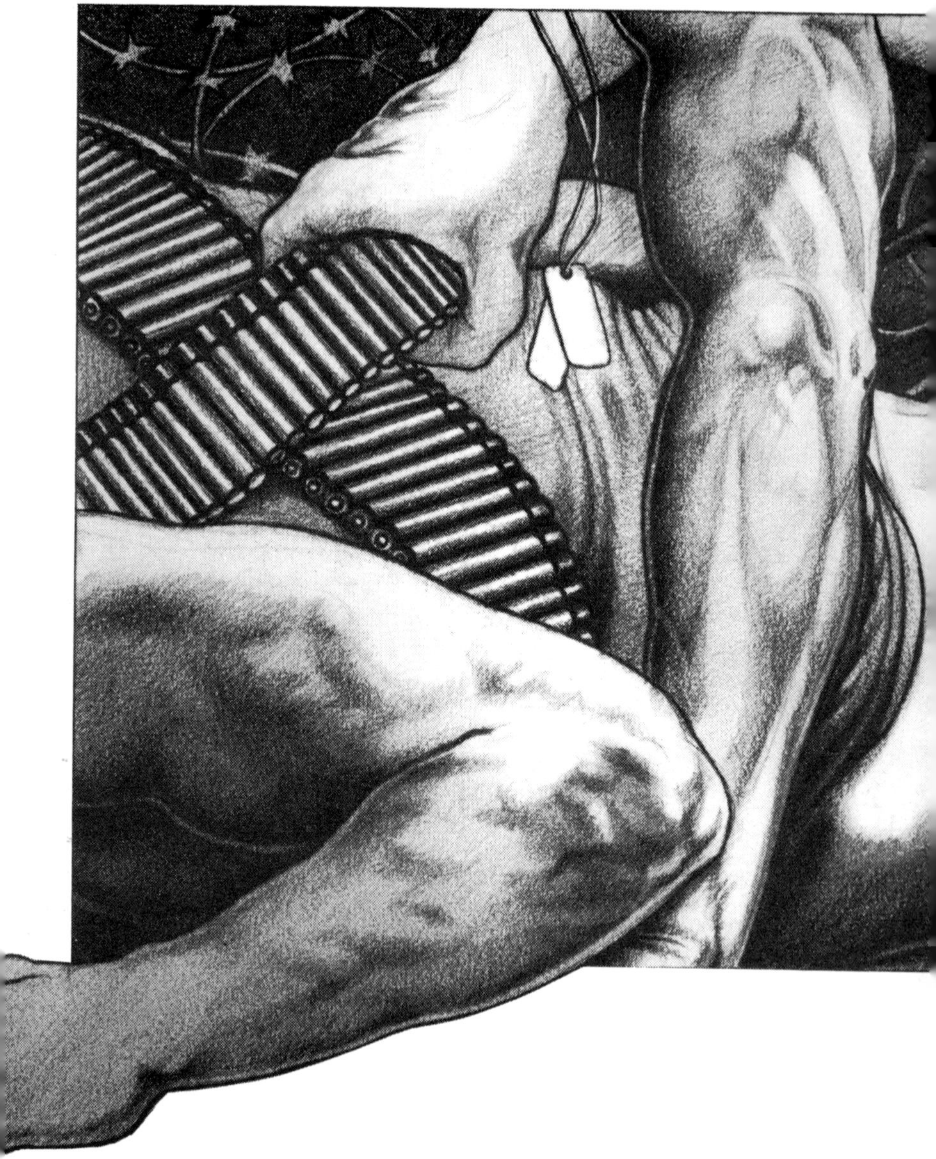

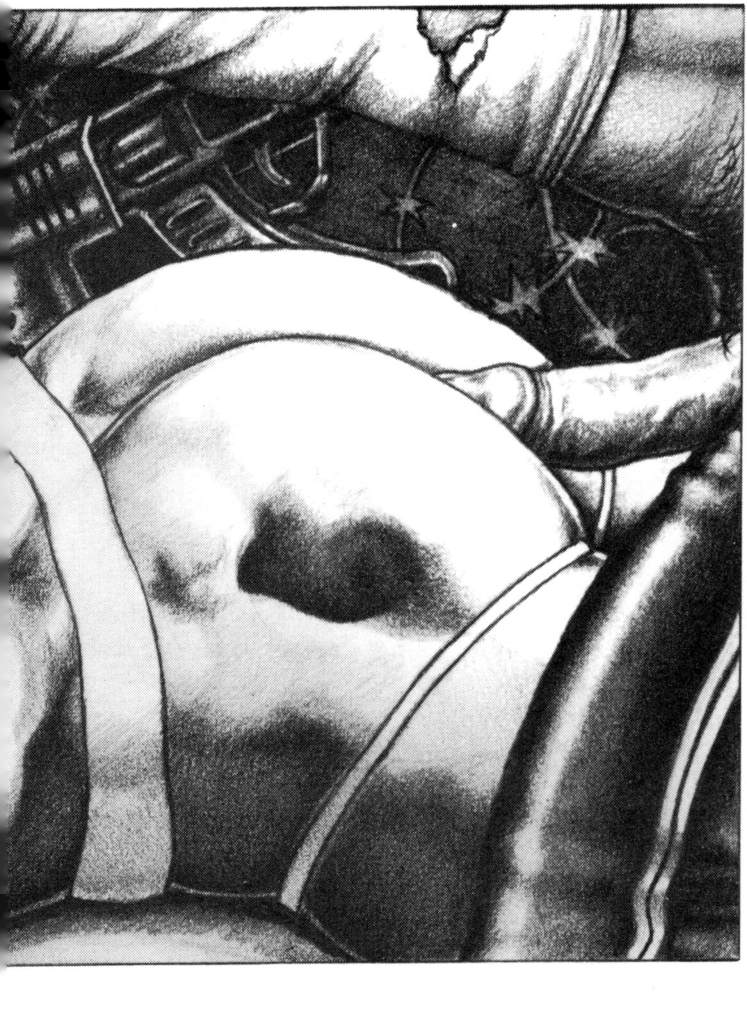

THREE

They had been away from their base three days and three nights and had journeyed further than planned when they came upon an oasis in the desert, an expansive farm fed by a broad aqueduct, which in turn fed a network of canals and orchards flourishing alongside. Before noon of the fourth day, they came upon a house, a rambling, three-storied mansion of stone. In the barn not far from it, they found twelve corpses, three of them children, no doubt the remains of the family and workers who had inhabited this wealthy estate. The three adult female bodies were nude, and by the arrangement of the cadavers Block judged they had been executed, each shot in the back of the head. Not likely by the enemy, as the Russians had never penetrated much of the country. More likely it was the work of some marauding gang. It was reported these were numerous, in caravans formed of motorcycles and jeeps; motley gangs of thugs and their chicks in search of provisions, gasoline and money, raping, torturing, murdering those they looted. The victims here must have been taken off guard by a large group, rounded up swiftly without much struggle and shot like dumb beasts. Not by a well-organized gang, for, investigating the ransacked premises, the soldiers saw the raiders had taken no more than they could carry on their backs. Left behind in their inexplicable haste were goods and valuables aplenty. "Perhaps they'll be back," Bain said.

Block's men needed a rest, and he decided they would not bury the bodies until the following morning, so the barn doors were shut. A sentry with binoculars was stationed atop a silo. The next step was to find what food the place afforded, for the volunteers had been eating rattlesnake and jackrabbit for two days. The murders had probably taken place the day before, for a gasoline fueled motor was still running, and it turned the generator which supplied electricity, and the contents of a deep-freeze locker would supply more than enough for several meals for the lot of them. Marshall and Holmes took charge of the kitchen to prepare a feast. Several men returned the luxurious living quarters to some semblance of order, willingly, for it had been a long time since they had known anything of domesticity and none had ever seen a house as elegant as this; the living room with soft, velvet upholstered furniture, ornate goldleaved, marbletopped tables, potted plants and an art gallery of flamboyantly colorful paintings. Racked wine bottles were found locked behind a heavy door in a subcellar along with a cache of gin, scotch, whiskey and rum. Block had decided that this was where he would bring his purpose to ultimate fulfillment and gave permission for the booze to be passed around to those who cared to get drunk, "roaringly drunk if that's what suits you." While meat thawed in a microwave before cooking, the drinking began, and the men doffed their dust-sweat caked tunics. They dove into the swimming pool, and groups of four took turns enjoying a steaming bubblebath in a jacuzzi, their drinks at the ready on the surrounding tile coping.

Retiring alone to a room upstairs, Block felt more and more like some obsessed Ahab, although what drove him was not a need to be avenged. He had no need to sail halfway around the world to slay a white whale but was determined that here, in this famrhouse, the white semen of all his men would be mingled in a Spartan bonding. Hypocrisy had been broken down. During the three nights since the cloudburst there had been rough lovemaking in pairs, here and there a threesome. Before dawn that morning, he had arisen and wandered among his men, some still asleep, some beginning to stir: Tullius and Gerald nestled together in a narrow hollow; Marshall with the Black; McCormick with Vild; Kinsbursky with Dunning and Rappaport. He himself had spent two nights with Dimick, Riley and Saunders. However, the wedding of all these men wasn't yet complete, and there were still some obstacles to be overcome. Saunders had shied away from sucking or being buggered. Dimick finally took it up the butt but couldn't bring himself to go down on a comrade. And, until Tullius reciprocated and blew Gerald, Vild allowed himself to be buggered by McCormick, the circle would be incomplete. Each must go the full course with each, Block said to himself. They are horny enough, and it's all very well that we had ourselves a rambunctious orgy in a cloudburst, but what is needed is something more orderly—regimented lovemaking, each giving and each taking with all. general lovemaking, each giving and each taking with all.

That morning at muster, once again the officer has begun to perceive the formation it would require. Marshall had the unit at calisthenics in two rows, first doing knee bends, then bending over and touching toes. While Block had moved from man to man down the first row, he'd asked each to stop still when bent over, so the crack of his ass and anus could be inspected, most of them puckered tightly and resisting the pressure, a few wincing. He'd done the same down the second row of assholes, one cherry red, most dirty brown and hair covered, two almost hairless and each one a primordial portal to the far side of each man's psyche. After he'd moved from the last volunteer in the muster of twenty, he'd returned to the first, turned around, bent forward, pulled the mounds of his butt apart and announced, "I expect each of you to have at it, beginning with you, Bain. Have yourself seven or eight strokes and then make way for Bartollata." Not one of his men had failed him, and, while being sodomized by first one and then another and another, he'd felt as if he were a creature apart from his usual self, a stranger adrift in foreign space, someone he didn't need to understand or rationalize, someone who simply existed. "I am fucked, therefore I am," he'd murmured. Six or seven of the volunteers, the hastier comers, had climaxed in him, his rectum awash with semen. "They come, therefore they are," he'd muttered.

A spectator had said, "Jesus Christ ... this Block doesn't fool around."

"He's no sissy."

"He's a champ, man . . . a living, breathing champ."

Later the colonel hotly thought, I have set the example and expect each of them to have done unto him what they have done unto me . . . in order to make the bonding complete. If comrades can go up over the trench and charge no-man's land in the Somme and be mowed down by machine-guns together, they can do anything. All that is needed is the correct formation to rally them.

Upstairs in the house, the room he went into no doubt recently belonged to one of the deceased children: on the walls were drawings of fantastic animals, a cat with the wings of an eagle and the face of a monkey, a zebra with the neck and head of a giraffe and reindeer's antlers. He mused, if I hadn't become a soldier, the next best thing would have been a painter. What magnificent visual worlds they have created. While soaking in a bathtub in an adjacent room, he thought, I would have been an impressionist, a cubist, symbolist and abstractionist . . . and what incredible paintings one might achieve of twenty-two naked, horny, strapping men all trying to achieve physical accord. What a variety of couplings might be made until, at the last, the final, resolving one is hit upon. I will find it.

He was exhausted, and soon his head fell forward, its chin on his chest, and he slumbered. How long he didn't know, except the water was cool when he awoke and the light in the room was that of afternoon. He returned to the bedroom, considered the pictures on the wall again, one of an elephant with the head and face of a man. After sitting on the floor, he took a yoga position, the soles of his feet placed together, his heels close in, and for a while, he concentrated on his breathing, nothing else, until consciousness was reduced to an essence. His distilled meditation then turned to one thought—of how he would consummate the marriage of his men, of how each would be both bride and groom to all in a close-order drill, in equality and interwoven conjugation.

From an open window laughter briefly buoyed in the balmy air but the colonel paid no attention to it while he once again considered the fantastic shapes on the walls. He remembered the abstract paintings he'd seem when a lad and remembered the delight and awe he'd felt in the liberation of his senses, the artists having altered the ordinary, literal manner of perception and created in riots of color a world of intriguing shapes and impressions, giving new sight to eyes. The world outside the galleries had never been the same again. And what had been true of these paintings for him had also been true of gazing close up at a marine sergeant's cock and balls. this had altered his perception of men forever, just as seeing Lyons' decapitated torso impaled on a stake had forever changed his feelings for the men who served with him. Lyons! Lyons! I loved you. Oh God, how I wish we had wedded.

In time, Block's mind resubmerged in a self-hypnotized state, and what was conjured up was a vision of Sergeant Lyons, seen after his torture and death, his head on a stake, his blood congealed at the severed neck and his torso raised on another stake. The corpse, rather than bloodless, was flushed red, glimmering in its sanguine nakedness. Block imagined himself rising and crossing over to the sergeant's remains, withdrawing the bamboo slivers which had pierced his eyes, cheeks and genitals; kissing the dark eyebrows, then the mouth, which was not cold, but warm and supple. Feeling it kiss in return, he whispered, "Did you guess that I was falling in love with you?"

Without lips moving on the face, an answer welled up, "Yes."

"Two days before you died . . . when I saw you bathing in a lagoon . . . I was awed by your brawn . . . and your vulnerability, too. Did you see?"

"I saw."

"Would you have helped me to learn how to love you?"

"Yes."

"How would we have loved?"

The cock on the headless torso arose, and kneeling before it, at the altar the crotch was, the colonel remembered phrases from a requiem mass: *laudamus te, benedicimus te, adoramus te, gratius agimus tibi, glorificamus te.*

"Do you know...that because of you...in honor of my fledgling love for you ... a love cut short ... I have sucked five hundred cocks and will suck as many more if I live to do so ... and will drink as much cum as will be given to me?"

"Do it."

"In honor of your death."

"No, of my life."

Block's lips caressing two-thirds down the length of the phallic eucharist, he murmured, *"Laudimus te."* Then he asked, "Have you read what I have in mind for my men?"

"Yes."

"And?"

"Do it ... in honor of all soldiers who should have but didn't love one another in time."

"Would the world be different if they had?"

"Maybe yes ... maybe no ... but we would have had the glory of doing it."

"You wanted me to love you?"

"Yes."

"Had I known, events might have gone differently. I might not have sent you out as forward scout. You might not have been captured and ...."

"But, as it is, you have me."

"No. You are dead, and I lost you and have grieved for you. I can only hallucinate you."

And Block did. His head glided back and forth succulently, saliva plentiful, an overflow dripping onto and then from the skin which sacked Lyons' testicles, *adoramus te,* the organ enveloped by his mouth growing longer, broader and heavier in its rigidity, the orifice expanded to accommodate it, *glorificamus te,* the sheltering room falling away into oblivion until there was no surrounding desert, no earth, no interstellar heaven, only the coupling of man with man in bountiful fellatio, a Milky Way presently gushing forth.

By the time Block had come from his self-hypnosis and by

the time he had risen, left the room and gone down the stairs of the large house, he had clearly visualized what formation he would ask his volunteers to take that evening.

They had feasted and shared liquor. Five sat at the long, cleared dining table under lamplight, playing poker, gambling red, white and blue chips found in a chest of drawers. Three smoked cigars found in a cannister. Two of them sat sideways on their chairs letting what cross-ventilation there was cool their crotches. Saunders wiped sweat from under his scrotum, his flaccid dong flopping from one side to another. Outside on the long porch, three men, in the dark shadows of faintly stirring willows, were taking bets on the farting contest Ferguson and Dimick engaged in. Just as Block stepped out, Ferguson bent over, cheek spread, letting out a long, grinding fart, which changed pitch three times. Kinsbursky squatted a distance from the buttocks using a Polaroid found in the house to get a shot of the fluttering asshole. When the photo developed, it was given to Ferguson, who looked at it with something like fatherly pride. Then Dimick bent over, breaking wind, the flashbulb illuminating his big, round, almost black anus. Beyond, in the yard, three nude soldiers dribbled a basketball among themselves and took practice shots at the overhead ring in the fading light. As soon as Block let his presence be known, these men, as had the card players in the dining room, came to attention, not indifferently, but with alacrity in spite of near inebriation. He asked them all to gather in the dining room. After Marshall had rounded up those who were missing, including the sentry, Block proceeded with his plan. Rather than brief them on their coming mission, he told them what was expected of them in the next hour. Using as few words as possible, he explained the formation he wanted them to take, using the same tone of voice he would use to explain a maneuver in a skirmish with an enemy. If any of the volunteers wanted to balk at the challenge presented, none spoke up with objection. But each man's test would come when it was his turn to get up on the table and take on, one by one, all twenty-one studs: just as the true test in a battle came when soldiers saw the tide had turned against them and there was nowhere to run. He expected the best of them, and they knew it. They expected it of themselves.

So it was, at last, to be begun; the wedding rite, to be accomplished, to be fulfilled.

≠

Within a month they had been flown halfway around the planet, had parachuted into a region above the Khyber Pass, west of the Himalayas, near Kabul, verging on the Central Steppes of Russia, and there they joined with Pakistani and Afghan guerrillas in rough, arid mountain passes. Within a month of intermittent combat with the enemy, they'd lost one volunteer, flatulent Ferguson, who had been pulverized by an exploding shell after having gone the extra mile venturing to capture a deserted tank. There was not much left of him to bury.

Their mission was to disrupt a Russian stronghold, to destroy its intelligence and ammunition center if possible, or at least to divert it from joining a full scale engagement which would be begun a hundred miles to the west, although only Block was aware of the overall strategy. The chiefs of the two guerrilla groups, which numbered at least two hundred fighters, guessed the colonel must be privy to a master plan, for he had set up a timetable for their forays, focusing on a specific date a month hence, but neither chief asked what exactly he knew. It was best not to know too much, for those captured would be tortured. In spite of their fierce independence, the Muslims accepted Block as their intelligence officer and, as yet, couldn't fault him in prowess and valor, nor on his genius for tactics. Nor could they fault the men who served him as warriors; in skirmishes with the enemy they had proved to be as brave as any Muslim. However, they were in contempt of how the Americans flaunted their nakedness, wearing clothes only to protect flesh from the sun's glare, twice having fought the Russians in the nude. And these foreigners were compulsive bathers, rushing to any watering hole they saw, not merely content to clean off the day's grime but also horse-playing and making a display of their sexual arousal. The Afghan chieftan had told the American officer this was a crime against God and his people's law demanded punishment for such behavior, and if any of his men ever committed such obscenities they would be driven from the clan. Block, in response, asked, "Who is your God?"

"He is Allah ... the one and only."

The two men spoke through an interpreter with only the light of the full moon to illuminate their faces, the surrounding night intensely silent.

"Does your Allah write down laws?"

"He has instructed his prophets to write the laws."

"Have prophets written that men should not share their sexuality ... written this in so many words?"

"It is written that men should be chaste."

"But surely your men take wives."

"A man may father offspring without serving lust. It is written that men should not lust after women either. He should perform his manly function but not linger with women ... not even his wife."

"Is that too written in so many words?"

"It is the custom of our people."

"But aren't customs manmade ... and not the will of an unseen God?"

"Allah makes himself known through virtuous men."

"To what purpose?"

"To serve him."

"And to wage war?"

"It is not we who make war. It is the enemy which has invaded our country. It is the enemy who seeks to enslave us and thereby destroy our customs. A virtuous man must be free and cannot serve foreign tyrants and Allah at the same time. Just as a man cannot serve lust and Allah at the same time."

"Does your religion admit that men, by nature, are prone to lust . . . particularly young men, such as the many in your ranks?"

"Young men are to be instructed by their elders . . . and their virility must be molded to the will of Allah."

Block had been unable to guess Amid Mohammed's age. The lean, bearded face of this turbaned fellow had been weathered by hardship and exposure to harsh elements. Nothing had been seen of his body, since he wore a coarse, bulky robe over his heavy trousers, although the cinch of the belt around his waist indicated that he was a thin man, one almost six feet in height. As far as the colonel knew, Amid had not removed his clothes in the two weeks since they had met, not even to bathe. Apparently Allah, unlike the Jehovah of Jews and Christians, didn't hold cleanliness to be next to godliness. Block smiled when he imagined what Amid's crotch must smell like; no doubt a camel, he thought, but was attracted to the man, particularly the stern set of Amid's jaw and mouth which contrasted his dark, soft, meditative eyes. But then the American was attracted to almost any warrior, and the sight of the many rugged, burnished Muslim faces aroused him daily, particularly when he allowed himself to think of all that hot, uncircumcised cock—probably dankly aromatic within that soiled garb. He had to suppress smiles when he saw these fellows at prayer, with their foreheads pressed to the ground and their berobed butts in the air.

However, he would make no move to seduce a single one of them and had told his men they were not to lay a hand on any Afghan or Pakistani, not even the youths who stole away from their own group at dawn and, hiding behind boulders, watched the Americans at their bawdy bonding rites. Block insisted, "No matter how excited they may become . . . even if they rush to join us . . . do not touch one. They are so ingrained in their austere customs and religion, they will hate us and themselves afterwards . . . and punishments will be exacted." As far as he knew, he had not been disobeyed, although he didn't know who copulated with who or what comingling there might be after the darkness of night settled over encampments. What the stars above see, is their concern, not mine.

While Block might question Amid's faith, he would not challenge it. "He and his men have distilled their way of life to an essence and drunk deeply of it . . . a potent brew which has drugged them," he said to Marshall. He believed each man had the right to fulfill himself as he saw best, whether it be with work, soldiering, art, lust or religion, or any combination. Which was not to say however that these guerrillas were not foolish—self-mocking clowns, he thought. Just as nature had given them legs to walk upon, hands and arms to labor and create with, eyes to see and ears to hear with, mouths to speak from and brains with which to think and wonder, so they had been given sensual flesh, excitable genitals, and to deny the profundity of mutual sexuality was to deny Creation as much as it would be to refuse to walk, toil, watch, listen, communicate or speculate. "A man should fuck as often as he can and cares to . . . with as many mates as he wants," he had instructed his volunteers. So, while on the one hand he honored Amid's decision to believe as he did, Block could not but hold that the man's strict religion maimed him.

Also, wasn't it likely Amid lied to himself? Surely the man had erotic dreams from time to time: nocturnal emissions, which would well up of their own accord in spite of his ego's denial of the lascivious; dreams which, even though forgotten, were part of him by the very fact that his psyche had conceived them. During their conversation, the colonel was on the verge of making this point and asking what images strayed in the man's sleeping mind, whether they were surreal enticements or more explicit, whether women figured in them or any comrade, particularly the two young men who attended him. But he kept this to himself and instead asked, "Aren't you a trifle curious to know what my God may be?"

"There is but one God...and Allah is His name."

"I must disagree. Man conceives God, not the other way

around. And I conceive of a God different from yours. Mine is an unworshippable, unknown force which has created galaxies upon galaxies in a far-flung creation of abstract matter, interspersed with vast stretches of meaningless space . . . most of it, except for this minuscule planet, inhospitable to man. Even neighboring Venus, which appears so cool from where we contemplate it, is engulfed in hot hurricanes a million times the heat and velocity of anything we can withstand. Venus and the absurd Milky Way are indifferent to virtue and chastity. They ignore devotion and prayer."

"This so-called knowledge is a waste and not the concern of Allah . . . nor should it be the concern of man. Man's proper concern is the study of Allah's will."

"Then you ignore what is around us . . . the tumult of nature's absurdities . . . billions of insects devouring insects . . . mighty sharks evolved to procreate and feed . . . in a frenzy of feeding . . . and man killing his own kind with regularity. If Allah is the creator, he has created an orgasm of life, which thrives madly to thrive. If Allah created the great dinosaurs by the millions, only to wipe them out in a catastrophe, why should he scorn the bonding rites of a band of men, who muster with ten assholes in a row prepared to receive ten assertive cocks . . . in a universe where our sun will eventually burn out . . . where a panoramic mosaic of stars, insects, sharks and the ghosts of giant reptiles mock us all?"

The interpreter didn't convey all this, probably not wanting to offend his leader, and Block smiled sadly, perceiving another absurdity—man's frequent refusal to fully discourse and reason. It was no doubt useless to debate further, so Block concluded, "If it was not Allah who created this abstract, absurd spectacle, then he is superseded by a more insistent force, its meaning . . . if it has one . . . beyond our logic and imagination." He rose from his haunches and stretched his arms while considering the full moon so intensely silver in the black sky it appeared brittle. He thanked Amid for his hospitality and tea and departed. Feeling quite mellow, amorous, as soon as he was well removed from the guerrilla encampment, he stripped despite an Autumn chill. He was eager to be with his men, who by now would be bedded down bareassed, in threes and fours.

No campfires had been built for fear of scouting planes. The canyon they held out in was so deep and narrow, no tanks could be sent in, and the Russians feared sending in troops, since anyone on foot could easily be picked off by riflemen on upper ledges. Once a helicopter had attempted to fly low between the many cliffs to strafe but, in one of its swings, had smashed against a cliffside and exploded, its crew dropping out afire like torches. Block's men had dutifully buried their charred remains the following evening, in honor of all soldiers. Another time planes had dropped bombs into the canyon but bombs from on high weren't effective against personnel, which could quickly scatter and find shelter in caves. The stronghold seemed impenetrable, yet no fires were lighted at night, and camps were frequently redeployed to keep the enemy guessing where they were. It was strange, the colonel thought, that reinforcements haven't been sent to the Soviet garrison. It may mean the campaign in the west has begun early. But he never underestimated any enemy. "They can always resort to dropping nerve gas on us," he'd told Dimick early that morning after their return from a night raid. However, it hadn't been the moment to worry about that, for his big-limbed, naked volunteers were forming to muster in a mist. No one had been lost this time, and happily fierce battle lust became friendly sexual lust in the foreplay of ass-grabbing, soon all eager to begin the close order, erotic drill, with which Block had wedded these hung, libidinous studs of the earth, men and men in ribald conjunction, each husband to all, each tasting the sperm of all.

Having left Amid, Block hurried to where his men would be nested for the night, their encampment a considerable distance from those of the Afghan's and Pakistanis', secluded in a convolution of crags, not that they wanted to keep themselves separate. They would have proudly copulated for all the world to see, but Block had insisted on this separation so they would not offend the Muslims. Therefore he had a walk of twenty minutes or so and had to go through a narrow, curving passage amid boulders. Halfway along, he found himself unexpectedly surrounded by a pack of men, and he instantly knew who they were in the blackness by their smell. They were from the guerrilla clans, and he quickly understood they meant him no harm, as one hand grabbed his and placed it on an erection jutting from parted robes and trousers, the skinned back head sticky against his palm. Block was sure its bearer was one of the youths of Allah's followers. Then two more were pressing him, hands feeling up his flanks. Since he had vowed not to comingle with these men, he tried to break away, only to find himself more snugly encircled, his hands being pulled to one hardon after another. Voices yapping excitedly in his ears, he didn't understand the words but the imploring tones left no mistake about what was wanted of him. He was forced to a squatting position, and a cockhead was shoved against his closed lips, the glans smelling of smegma. His impulse was to suck it clean, but he resisted as he felt he must in honor of the Muslims' faith. Then semen came in thick rushes, soon slithering from his mouth onto his jaws, while the ejaculating fellow yelped. Fingers frantically worked to pry apart his clenched teeth, and then someone was shooting wads into his right ear, onto his neck. Block could not help but laugh to himself with the realization that he need to do nothing—these studs having seduced themselves, he mused, their pent-up loads bound to fly. Hands pulled him upright and forced him to bend over, and an erection began a stabbing search for his anus. There was more yapping. His butt was slapped and soon was moist with cum, however, he kept his sphincter tight regretfully, thinking, Amid's religion is as absurd as the desert.

He didn't know how many had descended upon him but, when the attack had subsided and he was alone, judging from the quantity of male nectar clinging to him he figured there may be been as many as twenty. "Bucks will be bucks," he said aloud while massaging the seminal fluid into the flesh of his thighs and chest. "Amid, if he knew, would punish them cruelly . . . while I would marry them . . . have them greet the morning with my men . . . all to bathe freely in friendship and to fornicate by dawn's first gleaming with *esprit de corps* . . . to rejoice in man's strange fate."

The next day, Block learned that a spy among the youths had reported their crime to the guerrilla leaders and the culprits had been driven into the wasteland without provisions, water or weapons.

≠

Block fondled a captured Russian's ladened scrotum, its bearer a blond youth more than six feet high, with wide shoulders and thick thighs, more than two hundred pounds of hard weight. The Muslims would have shot him along with the six other Communists taken, as they burdened themselves with no prisoners and left the murdered to scavengers—Allah's will, no doubt. However the colonel moved quickly to spare the Russians and put them into the safekeeping of his men, who led them into the labyrinthian canyon. Afternoon shadows were dark at a cave's entrance, and the Russians, who were fearful of being killed at any moment, were told to strip, Block being fairly fluent in their language. When they hesitated in consternation, their belts were undone for them, their trousers and undergarments pulled down, their shirts unbuttoned and thrown back. The officer went down the line, considering their eyes, their different builds, the fair and the brown-skinned. Two fellows appeared to be wild Asiatics, but it was the strapping blond who looked the most naked of all, a bolt of smooth-skinned masculinity, "a hung clod-hopper is what we'd call him back home," one of the volunteers said. This Soviet soldier was braced for what he expected would come next—the worst. His fear didn't lessen when he felt his cock being stroked then licked. He looked about in utter dismay, seeing his comrades receiving similar treatment, wiggling, resisting. When he was asked to turn around and bend over, he shut his eyes and clenched his fists, trembling, thinking that he was about to be tortured, and his expression didn't change even when he felt his anus being kissed. The orifice was a dark-chocolate hue, and Block parted it, revealing a swirl of tissue the color of a pale plum. He was tasting it when the Russian lost control of his bowels and inches of turd, firm as terracotta clay, quickly shit out. Block managed to dodge most of it, watched it fall to the ground, watched two more emerge and saw the sphincter quiver after the defecation. He led the fellow away, got a canteen of water, washed the streak of shit off his cheek and then proceeded to wash the youth's butthole, giving it a thorough cleaning with a wet finger gliding on the inner tract. Then he zestfully rimmed the morsel, while pulling at the Russian's tightly puckered pecker.

The previous day Riley and Vild had died in battle, and their bodies had been lugged to a burial site. But among Block's men there was no hatred of the enemy because of this, for, as among thieves, there was honor among soldiers. The Soviet soldiers, following orders, had fought without treachery, so why shouldn't they, if agreeable, have their bodies excited, why shouldn't their manliness be heralded too, in honor of all warriors, living and dead, and why should they not be won over in bawdiness? However, this youth from the ranks of the foe was unable to understand what was happening to him through the night which followed. He'd never lain with either a woman or a man, with a girl or a boy, and his libido was as crippled as Amid's, Block was sure. As a lad Fyodor Romaniuk had seen his mother lay in the dirt with a strange man, had seen them grapple, writhe and couple in a frenzy which terrified him. He'd also seen his lout of a drunkard father beat his mother to death and afterwards seen his father taken away to a labor camp. Fyodor had been taken by the State to clean barracks in the Red Army, in time to become a soldier himself. His days and nights mostly consisted of long watches, drill and work. Little recreation was given to

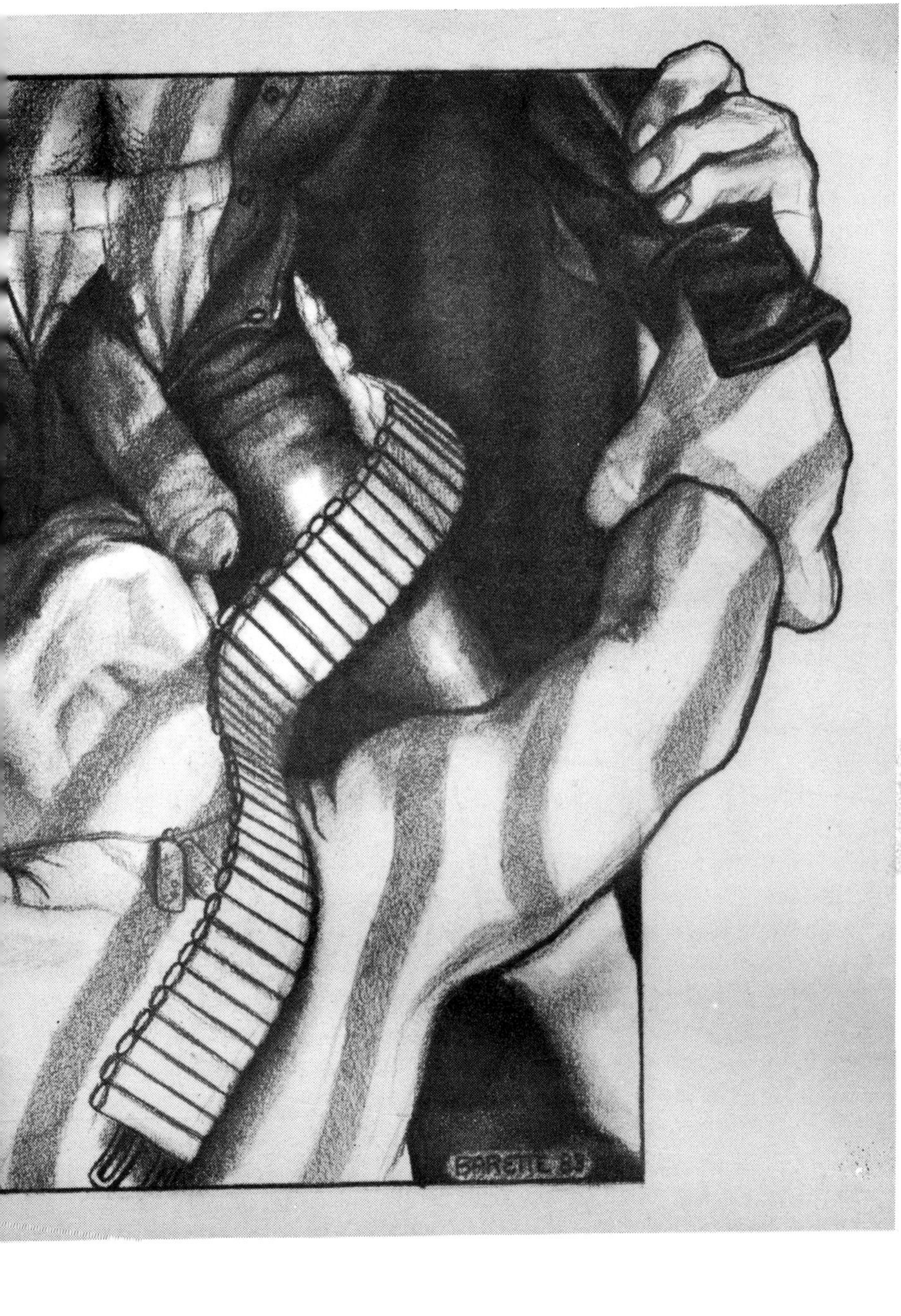

the troops, nor was there much humor among his comrades who were as backward as he, as constrained by regulations, taught to spy and inform on one another. So Fyodor had been dulled by tyranny. With the Americans, he still expected to be tortured or shot in spite of the fact that the officer had drawn him aside to lay naked with him, in spite of his body being touched and kissed. Perhaps he thinks I'm a lunatic, Block surmised.

Twice he told the husky fellow there was nothing to fear, that he should settle back and enjoy what was being done to him. However, Fyodor's legs and belly remained clenched, although in time his cock, being massaged and sucked, did elongate and thicken but without any hardness coming to it. In the middle of the long night, another voice was heard. "Has he come yet, sir?" "No." "Would you mind if I gave it a try?" "Be my guest." Another mouth, wetter and more voluptuous, was soon gliding upon Fyodor's member, but he still didn't know this was meant to give him pleasure.

He had once spent two days and three nights in pitch black, solitary confinement, brought from his cell from time to time for stern cross-examination, although he was never sure what his interrogators wanted him to tell them. Something about a comrade, who they said had deviated from the party line, but Fyodor knew nothing to tell, and the men threatened him with harsher methods to get him to speak up. Later he was thrown back into confinement, where there was hardly room for him to stretch. In the dark cave with the Americans, as they sexually worked him over, again he didn't know what was expected of him and feared the consequences if he didn't comply.

Finally Block said in Russian, "We'll leave you alone. Sleep if you can."

In the hours before dawn, Fyodor did manage a fretful sleep, often abruptly awakened by nightmares. Soon after daylight began to shimmer at the cave's entrance, he remained wearily awake, watchful of the men around, whom he perceived as dream figures. Standing nearby was one of his own countrymen, naked, an American kneeling before him, the Asiatic pumping away furiously into the others's face. Twice the cock slipped out, and the youth saw how rigid it was and how quickly the kneeling man got it back into his mouth, as if he were hungry for it. Of course Fyodor knew what it was to have an erection for many times he'd been startled from sleep by nocturnal emissions. He'd grabbed at the hardon and frantically tried to stop its spurting. If a dream had brought this on, he had remembered nothing of it and was ashamed of the mess he'd made in his shorts. However, several times he had rubbed his heavy, firm member back and forth over his belly and become cognizant of something approaching pleasure.

Presently, in the cave, standing above where he lay, his feet astraddle Fyodor, was a naked, blond American, who then sat on the captive's chest and smiled at him. The novice's eyes closed, and then Kinsbursky asked Block, "How do you say 'open your big, beautiful, blue eyes' in Russian?" The colonel translated, and a moment later they saw again just how splashingly blue the youth's eyes were, darting this way and that. "Settle down, you big-cocked horse. The way you act, you'd think we were beating you up instead of trying to make an asshole buddy of you." The nude sergeant looked to Block again. "Can you translate 'look into my eyes. I'm friend, not foe. So suck my nuts, you adorable hunk'?" After the officer did the best he could with this, Fyodor did take a look at Kinsbursky's face, as square-cut as his own, with eyes as blue, golden crew-cut hair, like his own, and the captive's gaze became quizzical.

"I look enough like you to be your twin, even if you are bigger. We're made of the same stock, you gorgeous Uke . . . so relax, babe . . . relax and kiss my dick." Kinsbursky, offered Fyodor a hand and spoke further, "Come on get up. Let's get you outside for some fresh air so you can get a gander at what red-blooded Americans do first thing in the morning." The light outside within the semi-protected encampment didn't dispel the big youth's impression that he'd awakened to a dream, where disrobed men limbered up, did knee-bends, stretched toward the sun. Some were talking, others silent still in grogginess, others laughing and horseplaying in a way Romaniuk had never heard or seen. He was reminded of young field animals romping in grass. This pristine morning no one was much concerned about enemy scouts, for on their previous foray they had seen that the Soviet garrison was being vacated, troops and truckloads of ammunition heading westward, no doubt on orders from afar. The guerrillas had managed to advance on this exodus in the dark and with riflefire, ignite the vans and blow their cargo skyward. While the garrison might not be completely disrupted, Block's volunteers were feeling victorious and reckless. They openly strutted their nudity, joked and grabassed, while food and water were passed. Before they were mustered for another celebration of their bonding, some men made their way to a unique latrine on the broad edge of a cliff, where there was a long fissure seven or so inches wide. Men stood, one foot on each side of the opening, squatted and let their feces fall to the rocks below. When Kinsbursky and Fyodor arrived, three fellows were using it, bare asses suspended.

"I don't know if you have to take a shit or not, kiddo ... but I do ... so watch." Taking his position, Kinsbursky called out, "One, two, three ... bombs away." Two turds dropped, and the broad smile he had on his lips brought a tentative smile to the Russian's face. "How about giving it a try! The cool air will feel great on the crack of your ass." The agile sergeant reached back and pulled the cheeks of his rump apart and then began a rocking motion. "Try it."

Fyodor had emptied his bowels the evening before, so nothing much came, but he imitated his teacher, at first cautiously, then with tentative playfulness.

"That a way, babe. Get that dong of yours in the swing of it."

And there they were, the two of them, hung and grown supple from the planet's clay, blond in sunlight, big of hand and foot, sturdy of leg, thick of chest and rump, and indeed they were like twins, brought together by a war which they could transcend. Then Kinsbursky pulled his companion to a more stable place, saying, "Okay, kiddo, I'm going to jack you off like you've never been jacked off before." He stood behind Fyodor, pressing abdomen to firm, curvaceous rump, and, with an arm around the youth's waist, got hold of the forward hanging cock and began stroking it, as lovingly as if it were his own. He spit on the middle finger of his free hand and began coaxing Fyodor's warm anus with the fingertip. "You're doing fine. This whang of yours is getting good and hard. Give yourself into it. You've got nothing to be ashamed of." He fully displayed the member to two onlookers, saying, "This stud's quite an addition to the family, wouldn't you say? Anyone want to come and suck on his balls while I jack him off?" Dunning did. Kinsbursky had half a finger inserted in the initiate's rectum and massaged the bulging prostate from within. "Come on, babe. You're gonna come ... gonna come."

And Fyodor presently climaxed, the first glob of his orgasm hurtling at random, but his cockhead was quickly brought to Dunning's gaping mouth. He felt that something was being torn out of his guts, and he cried out, almost screamed, as if the death blow he'd expected had been struck.

The following night, Fyodor slept with his new friend and learned what it was to embrace a fellow creature. Before this, however, he was initiated into the wedding rounds shared by the Americans. Three of the captured Russians, already seduced, joined in without a moment's hesitation, and the entranced blond also partook of the mass union, guided by Kinsbursky, who showed him what he must do step by step.

FOUR

A hundred and fifty years after, many young men of a clan were called Tom, and several of them may have been the great or great-great grandsons of Thomas Block. But this remained uncertain as the men who had settled in the mountain valley decades before had held women in common, not pairing with them, not creating families in the old way. So exactly whom the father of any one of many children was would never be known, and it was soon forgotten who the mother was, for the boys and girls of this community belonged to all and were reared in common. One old Tom was the chief of a council of ten, and it settled the affairs of the farmer-hunters. These people had known more than a century of peace and productivity in this fertile valley—ninety-two miles in length and forty miles across, ringed by mountains, with aqueducts to control the use of ample water, tilled soil, fields sown each Spring, harvest usually abundant; fruit orchards, heifers, steer, sheep, hogs and a variety of fowl owned in common, so there was always eggs, milk, meat, wool and hides. The young bucks of the tribe hunted game in the mountain forests, bucks who, the year round except in the worst of weather wore no clothes except footwear and cloth pouches to cup their genitals. These codpieces were only removed in the monthly orgy held among the males, although often when away from the village the youths paused in their hunt, dropped their bows, arrows and spears and fornicated with one another, imitating their elders.

None of the clan knew the outcome of a war which had raged throughout the world long, long before. But the memory of it was kept alive in tales, particularly one tale of a Colonel Block and his company of soldiers—the forefathers of this clan—and how with the help of guerrilla allies they had destroyed a Soviet stronghold. Their success had been in part due to the intelligence given by captured Russians. Due to a call for troops and material to join a battle to the west, the bastion had become undermanned and was an easy mark. After an ammunition depot had been blasted, the tale said, there was little left to defend, the surviving Communists fleeing in disarray beyond the western hills, never to return, although four Russians had surrendered to the Americans. The victors, in their canyon hideout, had waited one month before deciding their next move, on guard for any civilian or military movement, moving truck or airplane. But there had been none, and they came to believe they were cut off from the rest of mankind in this remote place, while the world no doubt continued to tear itself to tatters, destroying its civilization. Just as well, the men thought, since the old social structures had failed and brought on their own demise in a monumental suicide. They were free of it.

In the profound silence which followed the final explosions on the Central Steppe, Block and his men, all of whom had expected to die on their mission, understood they had been spared, if only for a time. Having found amongst themselves a new joy, they were only too glad to be out of the conflict with minds and brawn intact. They said farewell to their Muslim co-fighters, who were pleased to leave the sodomite Americans and head to the places where they had come from. However, fifteen young men deserted the Afghan ranks and sought out Block's band, eager to be initiated into the foreigners' carnal, godless ways. Seeking out a hospitable place to settle, the colonel had forty-five men in all to lead, eighteen of his volunteers, fifteen Muslims and eleven Russians, all lusty, so in their bonding rites there were forty-five rather than the original twenty-two. An Indian summer prevailed throughout October, and the pack went naked under fair skies. At night, around campfires, the men of different nations began to teach one another their separate languages. There was laughter and cocksucking.

Within another month the band came to a fertile valley and what remained of a farming community. They found among burnt-out cottages and barns, ten women and four children, who had survived the ordeal that had come to their village. Initially these females were terrified by the presence of these strangers who set up camp among the ruins. They remained in hiding, and Block instructed his men not to pursue them. "First, let them grow to trust us. We will rebuild their homes and put the village in order." His men set to work with tools found in rubble and with timber from the forests, the nude carpenters convivial in the waning days of Autumn, soft, slanted sunlight glimmering on shoulders, backs and rumps, laughter and horseplay frequent. When the laborers rested, they beckoned the women with smiles and waved erections, which brought blushes and bursts of giggles from the females. Seeing that the men were unashamed, they came from hiding with bared breasts and thighs. Seeing how the men flaunted their genitals, the womenfold did likewise, and Block saw that it was time for a mass wedding. There was game to be had from the mountains, the orchards had not been entirely ravaged of fruit, and coarse bread was made from grain which had been hidden away, so a feast was prepared for the nuptials. Block did not let his men fight over the women, did not let any man mate with a single female. All ten brides coupled with all forty-five grooms, and the women were delirious with the orgasms the men aroused in them.

The following August infants were born in the remote settlement. A year later the fold was increased again.

A disciplined leader, Block gladly accepted the responsibility for improving his people's lot. He did not write out tables of the law, but the members of the bucolic congregation were instructed on how they must live with one another.

The colonel had fought Communists for fifteen years and was often amused because now he chose to adopt a communal way of life, which his followers readily accepted. Nothing was to be privately owned, not wife, child, house, harvest or farm stock, not even a male's genitals was his private property. The shared sexuality was perhaps the essential ingredient for the success of this cooperative enterprise. Block understood, however, that men must keep and honor individual assertiveness, so he established regular athletic tournaments: boxing, wrestling, broad-jumping and javelin throwing, the hundred yard dash and long distance run. All this was done in sweating doggedness. And, since he knew men performed best when organized, he mustered and drilled them daily, even in the wind, rain and snow of winter, the men proudly accepting any challenge.

Before the onset of their second December in the valley, their leader had regulated the sex lives of the frolicsome band. A large communal house had been built for the women and children, another for the men alone and a third where males and females might lasciviously co-mingle—but no more than once a week. Also, in commemoration of the first wedding of the warrior-brothers, each month at full moon the grown men left the women and children, trekked to the foothills and in an expansive meadow repeated the rite Block had devised for them one desert evening on the other side of the planet, where, in a luxurious farmhouse—after the colonel had communed with the ghost of a man called Lyons—he had found his volunteers waiting for him and, after gathering them in a large, lighted dining room, had briefed them on his purpose, a purpose which had become like forged iron in his will, a purpose which they must set in motion.

Some of the men may have wanted to protest, to refuse. If so, they kept silent, just as men had done the bidding of officers when told to charge at Agincourt, Gettysburg and the Somme. Half were eager to begin. Sergeant Kinsbursky conceived of an added preparation, announcing, "Since I'm going to be fucking every last one of you, if anyone's got to take a shit, do it now. I don't want to get my beautiful pecker dirty." He got the douching equipment down from an upstairs bathroom, and Master-sergeant Marshall had pans of warm water brought out, so enemas could be administered. One butt after another took the nozzle. French doors were opened out to balmy night air, and men quickly darted out to squat and crap. Kinsbursky grew quite madcap, fingering asses as they were presented to him. "Hey, Rappaport, that's really a rosy red bunger you've got there. I can't wait to get into it."

"How about yours?"

"Have a look." This descendant of Ukrainians bent over and presented his fair anus, saying, "Give me a shot from that douche."

After the purging, Block, elated by the willingness of his men, was the first to get up on the long, oak dining table, the first to lay on his back, to draw his knees toward his chest and to present his rounded rump—to Bain, the first in line, who slipped in his greased erection for the seven strokes alloted to him before it was his time to get up on the table alongside Block. Bartolatta was next and, after he'd pumped seven times into Block, he moved on to Bain, who grit his teeth and braced himself. The colonel asked him if he'd ever been fucked before. "Only once, sir. A long, long time ago. And I was drunk."

"Well, there's always a second time," Bartolatta said, leering, waving his cock.

Bain snarled in response. "If you're going to do it, do it. Don't just stand there threatening me with that ugly thing." His eyes tightly shut when the hardon submerged, and he grimaced and grunted while being humped. Then his eyelids flew open when the buggerer withdrew, Bartolatta asking, "How did you like that?"

"Shut up. Get up on the table like you're supposed to and shut up."

When Bain had to take Dimick, he looked at the thick,

erect organ with alarm.

"You man enough to take it . . . like Block?" Dimick asked.

"Get it over with . . . fast."

"I don't think you want me doing it fast. It might tear this pretty, little asshole apart. Out of kindness, I'll take it slow and easy."

Two gobs of lard were applied to the orifice, and Bain stared at the overhead chandelier as he took the inserted mass. Beads of perspiration broke on his brow, and his grimaces were fierce when he took the cock's full penetration. The burly man was as good as his word, taking his time, pulling back, submerging his member, pulling back, sinking it again with deliberate care. "Man, you know you love it."

After Dimick had had his seven strokes, Bain exhaled explosively; his body sagged. "Whew! What a fucking sensation. I thought I was going to crap the whole world out." Looking at the next man, he spoke with fervor, "Get it while it's hot." By the time the eighth volunteer was buggering him, Bain's face was in repose, and when the twelfth cock was slipping in him, he turned to Block and shared a smile, almost cherubic, his right hand straying to and finding the officer's hardon. "I never thought it would be so good. I'd sure like to jack you off, sir . . . like to see you shoot a load all the way to the ceilng."

The fourteenth man was beginning down the line, the previous Spartans not having shied away from the dilated rectums offered them; however, when it came time to get up on the table and have done unto them what they had done to others, a few hesitated and grumbled. They were hissed and booed, one man yelling, "If you're man enough to stand and fight, then you oughta be man enough to lay back and get fucked," and then ten men were industriously sodomizing their comrades, the muscles of thighs flexing and unflexing in agitated abandon. Grunts and groans were heard along with the slurp-slurp-slurping. Block remembered the chop-chop-chopping of a helicopter in which men had bled and suffered rather than share their horniness and wisecracks.

"Shit, man, your butthole looks like a manhole with the cover off. Anyone ever get lost in it?"

"My daddy never told me I was going to be in an army of cornholers."

"Did you ever figure you'd get gangbanged under a chandelier, you homely bastard? Take my eight inches."

"By the numbers ... one, two, three ... fuck!"

"I'm fixing to go off ... so you're the lucky one. Here it comes. Jeeeeesus, take my load!"

"By the numbers ... one, two, three ... come!"

When the eleventh man had moved down the row and coupled with ten asses, he went around and laid on the other end of the table, drew his knees toward his chest and bowed his buttocks at the table's edge offering it to the fellow who followed. The latter in his turn took his place on the polished tabletop, as a second row began to form, one man at a time, flesh slapping, pelvises jarring. McCormick began ejaculating before he got his cockhead placed into Kinsbursky, however there was more to come after he thrust in his snaky member, the lanky, hirsute man standing transfixed in his orgasm. The sergeant's anal tract was well lubricated with grease and semen, so the next man, Owens, got in with ease. "Nothing better than hot asshole."

When it was Rappaport's turn to bugger Kinsbursky, his eyes gleamed with ferocity. "I've been wanting to fuck you ever since I first saw you."

"Why didn't you tell me? Think of the time we've wasted. Kiss it first and you'll like it all the better."

"I wouldn't kiss that asshole of yours for love or money."

"But you'll probably do it for the hell of it before this is over."

And so it progressed.

After he had received a hundred and forty seven thrusts, it was time for Block to get to his feet and begin down the first line of bare butts, some pale moons, some swarthy, a few hair coated, all beefy: down the first line of anuses, some brown, some crimson, the hair about them slick, all well-dilated.

Before interlocking with each, the colonel bowed to oral homage at each cock, each pair of testicles, each sphincter, like an administering priest before supplicants at high mass, except here the eucharist was the male body, Block enraptured before the inflamed, sensitive undersides of his hearty men: first Bain, *adoramus te*; then Bartolatta, *glorificamus te*; then Campbell. Each in his turn arose and followed their commander so that a circle of wedlock would be completed, *gratias agimus tibi*. When Block was sodomizing Ferguson, the man looked up at him suddenly startled, his voice urgent, "I hate to say this, sir ... but it feels like I'm about to take a huge shit." Block wasn't deterred and finished the allotted insertions, and immediately afterwards Ferguson got off the table and stiff-leggedly made his way to the open doors into the warm night, presently returning, all smiles, saying it had been a false alarm, "only a ripping fart." Before taking his place again on the altar, he bent over, pulled the crack of his rump apart and exposed his big anus in order to be plowed by the three men who had passed him by. Block, squatting before Holmes, lapped up a strand of semen which dangled from his steamy, black hole, the mass celebrated not with wine in memory of sacrificial blood spilled but rather with the milk of male loins in honor of living manliness.

The ballsy muster was momentarily broken when arrogant Tullius balked at getting on the table. Several of his comrades catcalled, one threw him into place, and Dimick sat on his face, anus to mouth, and brought the Italian's bent knees up, holding them securely, so that the man's rear could be primed. "Finger fuck this bastard. Don't spare the lard. Get two fingers in."

"Maybe what he needs is a fist."

"Don't kid us. You're queerer than hell."

Tullius was tamed, and the excitement among the soldiers heightened, several of the prone men pumping at the nearest crotches, fist and scrotums agitated, glimmering cockheads gyrating.

"Hell ... it's great being queer."

After Block had buggered all twenty-one, Master-sergeant Marshall last, he waited for Bain to finish his long round, then bade him to kneel and orally accept the erection held out, which Bain did as though mesmerized. Then this fellow stood to have Bartolatta do the same to him, then Campbell, then Dimick, a circle of fellatio begun, some hesitating before joining in, some closing their eyes as if in horror. They were cajoled and challenged. "You suck tit, don't you? So why not dick? Dick, tit...tit, dick." one said. If they could face death in a charge against an enemy of awesome power, why couldn't each face a row of cocks?

"You squeamish or something? Come on! Eat it . . . eat it."

"Everyone of us has wondered what it would be like sucking cock."

"By the numbers ... suck, suck, suck."

Gerald, crowned with golden ringlets, after savoring six crotches and before moving to the seventh, murmured, "God ... God ... do I ever love cock."

"No editorials. Just suck, babe."

In the lighted dining room, eleven men kneeled before eleven erections, faces mustered in slurping union, more than a few of the Spartans aroused to a second climax, one grunting and then announcing, "I'm fixing to come again . . . and it looks like you're going to be the lucky one a second time. Take my hot load!"

"One, two, three ... bust your nuts."

After each had tasted all, the dazed grooms broke ranks, some to sprawl on the carpet in near exhaustion and those with the livliest libidos to continue at lovemaking in twos and threes before sleep overtook them. Outside the farmhouse, six pranced nude under a desert full moon, their flesh gleaming like dark porcelain. The last two awake were Block and Riley, each with the other's testicle-filled, prickly-haired scrotum to his lips. After sunrise, all awoke from the slumber which had ensued with clear-eyed recognition of what had been done, of what had been shared—and they would never be the same again.

≠

In the fertile, mountain valley, this bonding ceremony was performed again and again, once a month, generation after generation. In time, the participants were three hundred strong, disciplined farmer-hunters, communal husbands and fathers—lovers too. Their children were taught survival skills: how to build, how to sow and harvest, how to stalk game, how to nurture domesticated animals which multiplied. Artworks adorned their lodge walls, the paintings depicted all aspects of their bucolic life: tillers in the field, women at the pottery wheel, youths hunting deer, children at play and men at their drills. Before he died at age eighty-seven, Block had twenty huge granite slabs dragged from a cliffside and erected in the meadow where the Spartan ritual was performed year after year. He had them sculpted phallic in shape and placed two upright rows of them, spaced a mile across, and, among these, set circular altars for the men of the clan to lay on, their buttocks and rectums at the ready.

Having abstained from sex for eight days, the males gathered naked at this site, good weather or bad, and at noon on the first day any young buck or bucks who had come of age, who had survived the tests of physical endurance expected of them, were brought forward, anointed with oil from crown to heel, their flesh and supple limbs painted with abstract designs, each with a special meaning passed on from one generation to the next. The initiates were rimmed, primed and sodomized by twenty fellows, in commemoration of the original volunteers. The youths in turn buggered those who had done so to them, while great drums were beaten and reed instruments piped, and another group of twenty, well-endowed men came up to a vat and, in mutual masturbation, shot their seed into it. These were followed by another eleven, who symbolized the Russians who had joined the Americans, and then, denoting the Muslims, fifteen men circled the vat in a mass jack, their cocks presently spurting. The issue of the forty-six was comingled with a fermented brew, this concoction ladled up and passed among the revelers. There were costumed pantomime shows, also running and wrestling matches, the winners later standing on a stage getting blown by the losers. Amid joking and laughter, there was a feast of roasted meat, bread and fruit. As evening settled in, great bonfires were built, and the nude men engaged in a free for all, their flanks and limbs glimmering, and, in inebriation, there was general fellatio and buggering under the moon and stars, under Venus and Mars, under the surreal Milky Way, "in an absurdly abstract universe," as Block had said.

But the rite had only begun. At dawn, the throng was mustered, to work up sweats in calisthenics, the athletes to prove their prowess on a long distance obstacle course, muscular men running, hurtling and rejoicing in their brawn. Later they bathed in a pond fed by a waterfall, comrades lathering and rinsing one another, scraping impurities from each other's skin, and there was much good-humored goosing. After, they gathered in an adjoining field, where they douched, rows of men mooning, rectums taking syringes which shot warm, oiled, perfumed water into them, rows of men squatting in defecation, and rectal tracts were reamed with greased, flaxen swabs until sphincters were dilated and glistening in preparation for what was to follow when the worshippers gathered at the altars among the phallic monoliths to being sodomy en masse, waves of robust exhileration rebounding among them. They formed in groups of twenty, and ten of one group shuffled with ten of another, and then another, so that carnal knowledge was further shared. Long ago Block had observed that men in their prime, men with hearty libidos, could have two or three orgasms any one day and very likely as many the next. He also knew the amount of semen produced by his band was bountiful, and that millions of vigorous sperms were produced in the lifetime of any one pair of testes. "The creative force gave us vastly more than is necessary for the fertilization of females," he had said to his followers. "We have an abundance to share with one another."

In the eighth generation, in the fever of any one of these revels, two hundred taut cocks plumbed as many butts; two hundred mouths lasciviously sucked at as many genitals, and it could be said there were at least six hundred ejaculations. Late afternoon of the second day found the weary celebrants strewn on grass every which way, much like fallen warriors had littered battlefields of old, but here they weren't riddled with shrapnel or oozing blood. Here their vital bodies were moist with sweat, saliva, oil and the sinewy nectar of their loins, some fellows asleep, some drinking and laughing. Here and there a tall stud stood jacking off onto the tangled limbs of several lovers who continued in indiscriminate, lackadaisical orgies until the hunger of male for male was once again appeased in sanguine accord. The mystery concluding one more time, several kissed the assholes of brothers in sleepy-eyed devotion.

In his ninetieth year, the year of his death, Kinsbursky had cackled an old man's laughter and said, "We sure had ourselves one hell of a fucking good time."

Thomas Block's last utterance had been simply, "Lyons . . . Lyons."

In the tenth generation, from over the mountains, came a nomadic band of misshaped people, almost dwarfs, paupers in tattered robes and with the vicious tempers of those who are hardpressed. Their flesh was gray and smitten with running sores, and they had wives, who were bedraggled, gnarled shadows of the males. Even if the natives of the valley had wanted to pacify these intruders, which they did not because of their ugliness, it became evident there could be no converting them, so it was decided they should be slain. However, the Spartans didn't move quickly enough, for the strangers carried diseases, to which the commune had no immunity. An epidemic raged, decimating its members. Intergalactic space took no note of their demise. The phallic stones were soon toppled. Rugged, wooden crosses were thrown up in their place. The universe was indifferent to the rantings of the people who worshipped a wrathful god. In time the galaxy would grow cold, unmindful of its fall into oblivion.

Block might have mused, Well, after all, it was only a cosmological, abstract painting.